THE
LAST NEPHILIM

Alexander J Boxall

J.A.Scott
PUBLICATIONS

Copyright © 2023 Alexander J Boxall

Published by J.A.Scott Publications

Front cover image provided by Canva

Back cover and internal photographs taken by A.J. Boxall

All rights reserved.

ISBN: 9798397077385

DEDICATION

To you.

For every time you forget how much you're truly worth.

Always remember:

You are stronger, more able, and more loved, than you
ever allow yourself to believe.

CONTENTS

THE LAST NEPHILIM

ACKNOWLEDGEMENTS

A special thanks goes to the following people who have helped in many different ways through the process of writing this:

Becky, for proof reading, pointing out inconsistencies, encouraging me, and putting up with me going on and on about it…

Jo Szedlak for being the first to read the start of my book and for giving me valuable advice.

Gill Tuck for being the first to read the whole book (and for giving me a review on her Social Media!)

Emily, Mim, Na, and Judah for not getting too annoyed with me when I kept vanishing off to write…

And everyone who's joined my mailing list in the lead up to this book's release – you have all been a great encouragement.

The Old Tree

PROLOGUE

The sun broke through the gap in the curtain, waking her up. He was still there, standing by the bedroom door. He was tall, strong, unlike anyone she had ever known.

Her eyes took him in, running over his smooth dark skin, following the contours of his shoulders, his scarred back, his strong legs, and she wondered what he had seen in her.

Only two days ago he had stumbled into her tavern, his clothes torn and stained with blood. Even then his dark brown eyes had blazed with a fire she hadn't seen before.

He had turned down her offer of a room, asking only for a drink, and by the time she'd returned with a goblet of wine, he had fallen asleep by the fire.

That first night she had stayed with him, tending to his wounds, the deep cuts to his arms, until she too drifted off, her head on his shoulder.

When she awoke the following morning, his wounds had almost entirely healed. Leaving him to sleep she'd tiptoed to the kitchen and prepared him some food.

They'd sat together at the table as he ate the Sabich she had prepared, the fluffy white pitta stuffed with crispy vegetables from her garden, and they had talked.

As she'd gazed into those dark brown eyes, she'd felt like she had known him her whole life.

They had spent the day together, talking as he quietly helped her with her daily tasks. He had no money so had insisted he be allowed to repay her for her hospitality. As he cleared tables and swept floors, things normally only a woman would do, she'd felt herself falling deeply in love with him.

That evening she had taken him by the hand and led him upstairs to her room where they spent the night together.

And now he was standing by the door, his back turned to her, shoulders slightly slumped as if a great sadness were weighing him down.

"I have to go," he whispered, breaking the silence, "my Master needs me."

His sorrow palpable, he walked back towards the bed, kissed her tenderly on the forehead, and as a single tear made its way slowly down his cheek he said: "Thank you for your kindness."

And with that he was gone.

A few months later, as the life within her grew and she was starting to show, she remembered the tenderness of his touch and the calm contentedness of his eyes. A quiet smile spread across her face and her heart was filled with peace.

She never saw him again.

CHAPTER ONE

Gabi Dos Santos was not looking forward to school. This happened sometimes. She loved learning, particularly science and maths, but today just wasn't filling her with joy.

It may have been the grey skies and the drizzle she could see through the window. Or maybe the way her aunt had burst into the room, opened the curtains, and greeted her with a cheerful "Morning Gabi! Time to wake up!"

Of course, it could be the fact she hadn't slept well at all, her night plagued, as usual, by nightmares that just seemed to get worse as time went on. Or perhaps she just didn't relish the idea of spending yet another day in that school, where you weren't popular unless you were sporty. And Gabi wasn't sporty.

"And it's P.E. today!" she groaned as she pulled her duvet back over her head.

She was just drifting off again when Rafa's voice woke her: "Come on, numbnuts! You're going to make us late!"

Rafa was her cousin, but they were more like best friends. They had grown up together after Uncle Mike and Auntie Em had adopted her, so she thought of him more like a brother than a cousin. He was only a few months older than she was, and had turned seventeen about six weeks earlier.

Her uncle and aunt had given him a car and a five-day crash course to teach him to drive. (She'd laughed at the thought of it being called a "crash" course…)

She knew she was going to be given the same course for her birthday in two months, on 7th July, but they were going to have to share the car, something she'd felt was a little unfair.

Finding her school uniform exactly where she had left it, in a crumpled pile on the floor at the end of her bed, she got dressed and went downstairs, flattening her unruly brown hair as she did.

Looking up from his iPhone, Uncle Mike greeted her: "Morning, Gabi! Ready for school?" He had a thick Brazilian accent that still brought a feeling of belonging to her heart. His real name was Michel, Portuguese for Michael, but when he had arrived in the UK as a teenager, with his sister, Gabi's mother, he quickly realised that "Michelle" was a girl's name and had called himself Mike ever since.

Gabi grunted, acknowledging his question, then sat down with the rest of the family and poured herself some cereal.

"Uncle Mike, can you write me a note so I don't have to do P.E. today?" she asked.

"Don't be silly," he replied, "Sport's good for you."

"But other sixth formers don't have to do P.E. It's just unfair."

"You know going to King Edward's was the one thing your parents specified in their will," Auntie Em interjected, "And I'm sorry if it has a different way of doing things, but it's a great school. At least you get to come home every day."

King Edward's was an expensive boarding school, just outside the village. It wasn't too far to walk but, since his birthday, Rafa had been driving them both to school every day.

Gabi and Rafa had been "day pupils" since they

started secondary school, aged eleven. Harriet O'Riley, Gabi's best friend, was a "boarder", so Gabi would often stay late after school, walking home in time for dinner, rather than getting a lift back with Rafa. She enjoyed the time it afforded her to think and be alone.

"Anyhow, why are you so grumpy today?" Rafa asked, "You on your period again?"

"Shut up, Raf," Gabi replied, "Not that it's any of your business, but no. I had a bad dream again."

She had been having these nightmares on and off for her whole life, but the last couple of months they seemed to have ramped up in frequency and intensity. She would sometimes wake up three or four times a night, clutching at the pendant that hung permanently around her neck - the only physical possession she still had from before her parents died.

Uncle Mike and Auntie Em exchanged a concerned glance. "What was it this time?" Uncle Mike asked, his voice less cheerful, his iPhone now locked and face down on the table, "Was it the usual?"

"I guess," she replied, "the usual mixture of darkness, and shadows." She didn't really want to talk about it but had learned, over the years, that actually telling her family about her dreams helped her see how ridiculous they truly were.

"I dreamt last night that I was being followed. I think I was walking home from school or something, I'm not entirely sure, but I was walking down this alleyway as it was getting dark, you know the one between Gordon Road, and Woodcroft Lane, and there was definitely someone following me. I even looked back, which I know you shouldn't do in a dream, but for some reason I did, and saw a man dressed all in black. He was walking at the same speed I was, smoking a cigarette. He had a long black coat on. I started walking a little bit faster and he did the same, then I started running and he started running too. Then the bushes and trees started changing into shadowy creatures all around me, and no matter how fast I ran, they were everywhere.

The last thing I remember is checking to see if the man was still following me but as I did everything around me burst into flames and I was surrounded by fire. That's when I woke up."

"Sounds like you're worried about something," Auntie Em said, "I'll get you some lavender oil for your pillow so you sleep better tonight."

"Sound like you ate too much pizza at dinner last night!" Rafa laughed, "You know cheese gives people crazy dreams!"

"Shut up Raf!" Gabi replied, punching him on the arm, "Anyway, isn't it time to go?"

She got up to get her school bag from her room.

As she climbed the stairs a feeling of dread came over her, as though something bad were about to happen. She hadn't felt like this since she was about six or seven and had to go to the bathroom in the middle of the night. She remembered how she used to wake up and see dark, evil faces in all her curtains, how she would lie in bed, too scared to go to the toilet, too scared to turn on the light. She must have been about nine years old when she realised that the "faces" were nothing more than shadows cast by the moonlight and that, by turning on the light, they disappeared.

Today, she had that same sensation as she walked to her room - the feeling that someone, or *something*, was watching her.

As she turned right at the top of the stairs she shouted: "Who's been in my room?"

No one replied.

They probably hadn't heard her.

Or were ignoring her.

She always shut her door, mainly because her room was her space and she didn't like the idea of just anyone walking in.

"I bet it was Raf," she muttered to herself, "he's so annoying…"

Everything appeared to be exactly as she'd left it, other than the window being open and the two pencils on the floor, which was odd as she always kept her stationery in a pen pot on her desk. Auntie Em must have opened the window for some fresh air.

She picked up her bag, tucked her hair behind her ear, checked the mirror to make sure she was presentable, and heard Rafa call up the stairs: "I'll wait in the car!"

"Coming!" Gabi replied.

Closing the door behind her, Gabi made her way downstairs. Halfway down she was sure she could hear her uncle and aunt whispering in the kitchen. Their voices stopped when she paused to listen, then: "Bye Gabi!" her uncle's voice called out from the kitchen, "See you after school!"

She walked out the front door shouting "Bye!" and got into Rafa's waiting car, ready to start the day.

CHAPTER TWO

"King Edward's School, Capel Cross is an independent boarding and day school for boys and girls aged 11-18. Our unique history and standing among British co-educational independent schools means we can provide the best preparation for adult life." At least, that's what the school website said.

Gabi wasn't sure if the part about preparing her for adult life was actually true, but it was old and definitely had "heritage".

As they drove past the red brick façade of the school, she found herself wondering how many people had been through those doors in the 450 years or so since the school was started. It was definitely an impressive building.

The front of the school must have been about 100 metres long, with three floors. There were seven windows per floor either side of the entrance arch, which was flanked by large pillars, two storeys high. Above the arch there was a turret, which at some point in time may have contained a bell, but now just had a statue of the boy king, King Edward VI.

That building wasn't even used for classes anymore, those were just offices for the headmaster, other teachers and the admin staff. It was a big school.

While the school was officially a "Church of England school", it definitely did not mean everyone there was religious. Far from it. She wasn't sure that any of the teachers were actually religious at all, other than the school chaplain, Rev Stevens, and maybe her Religious Studies teacher, Mr Ashdown.

What it did mean was that they had to be at school by 8:15 every morning for roll call, and twice a week they had to go to chapel, where they would sing hymns that made little sense to her, and where Rev Stevens would try to explain bits of the Bible to them.

Gabi didn't hate going to chapel, it just felt a little unnecessary at times.

Rafa dropped her outside her "house".

At King Edward's everyone belonged to a house. This was partly to make inter-house sports possible, but also so that the boarders would have a place to call home. Each house was twinned with the opposite sex, so her house "Aragon" was twinned with Rafa's house, "Henry", the boys' house.

With five minutes to spare before roll call, Gabi ran upstairs to her best friend's dorm.

Harriet O'Riley was sat on her bed and jumped up when Gabi walked in. She rushed across the room to give her a hug.

"You'll never believe what happened last night!" she exclaimed excitedly, her light southern Irish accent turning everything she said almost into a song, "There was a fire alarm last night, at 2 AM; all because someone, we all think it was Andy, set fire to the Oval."

The Oval was patch of lawn around which the boarding houses were built. It was oval, so it was known, quite unimaginatively, as The Oval.

"He didn't just set fire to it," she continued, "he actually wrote a message in the grass. I think he used petrol or something."

"What did it say?" Gabi asked.

"It was very odd, 'cos he hasn't been seen since, so I guess he's been expelled or something. He wrote

'Watch Out I'm Coming', which to be honest is a bit weird, but I heard Mr Foster, you know, the housemaster over at Henry, say something about him threatening the teachers, and how it was a crime, and that he shouldn't get away with it. I reckon he's definitely been expelled…"

After roll call, the two girls joined the crowds of students making their way across the campus to chapel. Everyone seemed to be stopping at The Oval to admire Andy's handiwork.

WATCH OUT I'M COMING

"I'm impressed with how neat it is…" Gabi laughed, as she and Harriet walked past.

Taking their seats on the hard, wooden pew allocated to pupils from Aragon House, Gabi started to relax, listening to the organ music being played by the assistant director of music as all the pupils walked in. It was always the same. She could have sworn he was making it up as he went along as she was certain she had heard snippets of Postman Pat and the Teletubbies theme tunes thrown in sometimes.

Her eyes wandered around the chapel taking it all in.

She'd been in there every Tuesday and Thursday since she'd joined the school six years ago, but old buildings still fascinated her, and this one even more so.

The chapel was designed like many old churches. Three large stained-glass windows at one end, directly above the altar, on which there were always two lit candles. In front of the altar was where the school choir sat, in rows of pews facing each other. On the end of each dark wooden pew were carvings with Latin verses and gargoyle-like faces. Gabi always thought this was an odd juxtaposition - the hopeful verses coupled with those monstrous faces.

Rev Stevens would normally preach from the raised

area between the congregation and the choir. This was where the pulpit was, on the left-hand side from where she was sat. The pulpit was also a little strange. Made entirely of wood, the preacher would climb a set of four steps into the circular platform, from where he or she could address the whole congregation. There was a lectern where the Bible, or sometimes the preacher's iPad, was normally placed. The lectern was decorated with a carving of a large pelican or stork that was plucking feathers out of its chest, drops of blood forming by its beak. All the symbolism was beyond her but at least it gave her something to look at while she was waiting for the chapel service to start.

The organ started up again, jolting her from her thoughts as everyone around her started singing one of the hymns she most enjoyed:

"Hobgoblin nor foul fiend
Can daunt his spirit
He knows he at the end
Shall life inherit…"

"Hobgoblins are so underrated," she whispered to Harriet, winking.

After the hymn, Mr Cox, the headteacher, stood up and came to the front of the chapel:

"Good morning King Edward's," he started, "As you are probably aware, there was a horrendous act of vandalism committed in the early hours of this morning. No doubt you were all woken up by the fire alarm, and you have most likely seen the damage caused to one of our school lawns."

He cleared his throat at this point, something Gabi knew was a sign of an extended angry rant. The headteacher did not disappoint her:

"How dare you?" Mr Cox continued, his voice getting louder and louder as his monologue went on, "How dare you desecrate the grounds of our beloved school? Our caretakers and gardeners work day and night to keep this place looking beautiful for you. For you! We spend literally thousands of pounds every month making sure this place is a fantastic home for every single one of you, and this is how one of you decides to treat our beautiful school? Disgraceful. Absolutely disgraceful." His voice suddenly went quiet, becoming almost a whisper, "I don't know which one of you did it. I have my suspicions, and I have called the police. But I promise you this: there will be consequences. Dire consequences. You have one chance. If you own up by the end of first break today, I will be lenient. But only if you own up by eleven thirty-five today."

A murmur rippled through the chapel.

"I thought they knew who did it," Harriet whispered to Gabi, "maybe they don't."

Mr Cox drew his angry rant to an end saying: "I don't need to tell you how important it is that we find the person who did this, so if any of you know anything, please come and tell me, or any of the teachers. We need to get to the bottom of this so we can make sure you're safe and that nothing like this ever happens again. Now over to Reverend Stevens who is going to talk to us about Jesus. Again."

Gabi chuckled at the way he said this. Maybe Mr Cox was bored of hearing the same thing in chapel every week too.

Twenty minutes later the chapel service was over and everyone shuffled out the building. As Gabi reached the door, slightly squashed between Harriet and a year seven boy who had somehow got mixed in with the girls from Aragon House, she turned and looked back towards the other end of the chapel.

Mr Cox and Rev Stevens were talking quietly just to the left of the pulpit, near the door to the vestry. Mr Cox was clearly very angry; his face was bright red.

As she turned away she didn't notice the shadow passing over the altar as one of the candles flickered and went out, leaving just a long tail of smoke drifting lazily towards the ceiling.

The School Chapel

CHAPTER THREE

Gabi and Harriet spent morning break together, in the library. They often did their biology homework at break time so they could have more time together after school, without the pressure of unfinished school work.

"Oh damnit," Gabi exclaimed, "I've left my calculator back at the house. I'll have to get it before my next lesson."

"Idiot! You better go, you've only got ten minutes. I've got English now so I'll see you at lunch. Enjoy your maths lesson!" Harriet laughed and added, "Don't be late!"

"I'll try!" Gabi said, looking back over her shoulder as she hurried out the library.

The quickest route back to Aragon from the library was through the admin block, through what everyone called "the Headmaster's Corridor." She rarely went that way as she'd have to go past Mr Cox's office. She couldn't think of any pupils who would choose to go that way, but she had little choice.

She pulled open the door at the southeast entrance and started walking down the long wood panelled corridor. The Headmaster's Corridor was always eerily quiet, possibly because it was away from the normal noise of school children and classes. Keeping her head down, she walked past the closed office doors, past all the school photographs that lined the walls, some of them dating as far back as 1911.

The corridor stopped at a door that led out into the space under the arch at the front of school. As she stepped out into the sunlight, she looked to her right and noticed a police car parked in the visitor spaces at the front of the school. It was just a generic white Ford Focus with blue and yellow reflective squares along the sides and the words Surrey Police written under a crest on the hood.

Mr Cox clearly hadn't been joking when he said he'd called the police.

Entering the second half of the Headmaster's Corridor, she immediately heard raised voices. Mr Cox's office door was slightly ajar.

Even though the thick carpet underfoot did a pretty good job of muting the sound of her footsteps, she slowed her pace a little so as to be even quieter.

As she approached the open door she could hear what was being said:

"...no, Mr Cox, that's not what we're saying..." a plaintive young woman's voice was saying. Gabi assumed it was one of the police officers, clearly not used to being on the receiving end of one of Mr Cox's tirades.

"What are you saying then?" Mr Cox was clearly angry. His voice far louder than it had to be, considering he was in an enclosed office and the police officers were no more than six feet away from him. "We've got a missing pupil, damage to school property, and my office was broken into and you're saying the only thing you can do is phone the hospitals to check if Andy's somehow ended up there? Is that really all you can do? Aren't you coming out to take fingerprints in my office? Do you think we haven't phoned the hospital to check if he's there? I feel you aren't taking this matter seriously at all."

"That's not the case, Mr Cox" a man's voice said,

"My colleague and I are just saying that's where we'll start. Can you explain what was stolen again?"

"Again?" Mr Cox sounded exasperated. "Only two things. The School Register which has all the names of all the pupils and teachers who have ever attended the school…"

"Don't you have those details on computer?" the young female officer interrupted.

"Of course we do," Mr Cox replied, "but this is an historic book. It's kept in the safe and passed down from headteacher to headteacher and is part of our heritage as a school. It was started by King Edward VI himself when he founded the school. It's priceless."

"Ok, what was the other thing you said they took?"

"A map. I had a framed map of the school. It was from 1783."

"I presume that's priceless as well?" The male officer asked.

"Of course it is, but that's not the point." Mr Cox sounded like he had just about had enough. What he said next made Gabi's heart skip a beat and her blood run cold: "The map was drawn by Ravi Dos Santos, who was a headteacher here in the 18th Century. One of his great-great-great grandchildren is a pupil here at the moment. The map shows all the secret tunnels that run under the school that were used during times of war to keep the children safe. It's of enormous historical value."

"Right…" the officer said, clearly not as concerned as Mr Cox was, "I think we've got what we need."

The door started to open and Gabi ducked into the doorway of the next office down to avoid being seen.

As the two officers walked down the corridor away from her she heard the female one say: "He seems more worried about an old book and an old map than he does about the missing boy…"

The officers stepped out into the sunlight at the other end of the corridor and Gabi ran in the opposite direction, past the entrance to the staff room and across the car park to Aragon to get her calculator, her mind filled with questions about her great-great-great-grandfather.

She was definitely going to be late for maths.

Elsewhere, Andy woke up. It was dark and the air smelled of old books. It was that musty smell you find in places that have been damp and dried out slowly, leaving behind the odour of mould and rotting wood. He couldn't move his legs.

As his eyes grew accustomed to the dark and the fog in his brain started to clear, the pain in his hands came into sharp relief and Andy cried out.

"Silence!" said a voice in the darkness.

"Wh-who's there?" he stammered, fear starting to spread as he craned his neck to see where the voice had come from.

No reply.

A darker darkness seemed to surround him and panic started to rise as Andy's heart started beating faster and faster, his burned hands now the last thing on his mind.

His instinct was to protect his head from whatever this thing was, but his arms were pinned down, as if anchored to the ground by an enormous weight.

Then the darkness poured in, invading every pore. He could feel it enter his eyes, his nose, his mouth, spreading down his throat into his arms, his chest, creeping up into his mind.

His eyes closed, he tried to scream as his heart stopped beating.

His body lay still and, silent, gave in to the darkness.

CHAPTER FOUR

Gabi couldn't wait to tell Harriet what she had learned. At lunch, as they sat together in the school dining hall eating their tuna pasta bake, the standard fare for a Tuesday lunch time, she started telling her what she had heard in the Headmaster's office.

"So you had a great-great-great-grandfather who was the headmaster here?" Harriet asked, incredulous.

"Apparently so. And he created a map that showed a whole load of secret tunnels under the school!"

At this point, Rafa came up behind Gabi and leaned over smiling: "Ready for your run this afternoon, ladies?"

Before she could say anything, he sauntered off to join his friends.

"Douche," Gabi laughed.

He was right though. They did have a run that afternoon. Every summer term during double PE, Sixth Formers had to go for a cross-country run. It was only a three and a half mile run but Gabi absolutely hated it.

She had never been particularly sporty and hated the fact that all the pupils who were good at sport got given prizes for academic work at the end of the year. They were also the ones who always got picked for the roles of head-boy and head-girl, while people like her and

Harriet were almost always overlooked.

"Shall we do our usual?" Harriet asked.

"Absolutely," Gabi said, smiling.

The two girls got changed into their PE kit; black shorts, a green t-shirt (the colour for Aragon House), and trainers. They joined the other girls in their year by the Cricket Pavilion on Upper Deacon. Every one of the four sports fields in the school was named after someone important.

Upper Deacon was right next to Lower Deacon. The other two fields were called Gurdon's Field and Brook. There were footpaths that ran around each field into "The Woods", a large wooded area within the school grounds.

One of the benefits of the cross-country run was that they actually got to leave the school grounds. The Cross-Country was a circular run that started by the Cricket Pavilion, took them past Gurdon's Field, up "Lover's Walk", a footpath that took them out of the school grounds onto Brook Road, then left in a large loop that went through the village of Capel Cross, up a steep lane leading away from all the houses, through some farmers' fields (with permission, Gabi assumed), along some footpaths, through some woods, then back down Lover's Walk into school, ending up right back at the starting point.

It was also a great route for skiving off, if that was what you really wanted to do.

Gabi and Harriet set off together, staying towards the back of the pack of runners. As they came out Lover's Walk onto Brook Road, Gabi stopped and bent down, while Harriet jogged on the spot next to her.

One of the other girls ran past and said: "Are you OK?"

"Yep, just doing my shoelace," Gabi replied, "We'll catch up!"

They waited until the other girls had turned the corner onto the main road into Capel Cross then sprinted down a footpath opposite Lover's Walk, straight down to Capel Cross train station.

At the bottom of the hill they slowed to a walk, enjoying the sunshine and the fact they wouldn't have to do the run.

"Half an hour?" Gabi asked.

"Sounds about right," Harriet replied. It was roughly how long it took most people to get back to Lover's Walk, so they would rejoin the run at that point.

Capel Cross train station was very small, with only two platforms. Platform 1 went to Guildford and then onto London, and Platform 2 went to Portsmouth. Each side of the station had a small shelter where people could sit and wait for their train, but the station was normally completely empty. Except on Saturdays.

Every Saturday lunchtime there would be hundreds of King Edward's pupils standing on both platforms waiting to catch the train either to Portsmouth if they lived that way, or to Guildford to go shopping.

Being Tuesday, as expected, there was no one there.

The two girls crossed the footbridge to the other side of the station and went into the local shop. Unimaginatively called Capel Cross Shop, it sold everything from magazines and newspapers, to chocolate, to Costa Coffee (from a machine), to toilet roll.

Gabi bought a Latte from the machine, a can of Diet Coke, and a Cadbury's Twirl while Harriet, as usual, just bought a coffee.

They walked out the store with their purchases when they were startled by a gruff voice:

"Got any spare change?"

Sat on the floor, next to the door, was a man. He had grey hair and a weathered face and was smoking a sad looking "rollie" - a hand rolled cigarette. He was wearing a long black coat over a t-shirt that said "Faith No More". Gabi recognised the t-shirt as Uncle Mike had CDs by the same band. The man's jeans were torn and dirty and he was wearing chunky big black boots that weren't laced up properly.

The two girls hurried past him onto the train station platform.

As they sat down, Gabi said: "That poor man. I'm going to give him my chocolate."

She left Harriet on Platform 2 and went back towards the shop.

"Here," she said, her hand outstretched holding out her chocolate bar, "I haven't got any cash but you can have my chocolate bar."

"Thank you, child," the man said, "I'm also very thirsty though."

Gabi hesitated for a second but then handed him her can of Coke.

Without warning, the man grabbed hold of her wrist and pulled her down towards him. She stumbled but kept her footing.

He was unbelievably strong and she couldn't pull away.

Before she could react, he whispered: "You should be careful. The world is more dangerous than you have ever imagined."

He released his grip and Gabi ran. She grabbed Harriet's hand saying: "Come on! I'll explain when we're back."

The two girls ran back up the hill, just in time to rejoin the rest of her year group as they returned to Lover's Walk.

The run finished back by the cricket pavilion and their teacher, Mrs Todd, an athletic woman in her mid-thirties who always had her hair in a pony tail and ran everywhere, pulled them aside: "Are you two ok?" she said, "You look pale as a ghost."

"I'm OK," Gabi said, trying to catch her breath, "I think the run just took it out of me today."

Harriet nodded her agreement and Mrs Todd said: "Well, it's nice to see the two of you putting some effort in for once. Now go shower and get changed."

As they walked back towards Aragon, Gabi told Harriet what had happened.

"I can't believe he did that!" Harriet exclaimed, "Especially when you were being so kind. It's so creepy."

"I know. I can't even tell Uncle Mike about it cos he'll tell me off for skipping PE"

"Can you tell Rafa?" Harriet asked.

"Probably. I'll tell him this evening. I don't really want to think about it at the moment."

"That's fine. Are you going straight home now?

"I don't know," Gabi replied, "I'll have to see what Rafa's doing. Why?"

"I was just wondering whether you wanted to try to find out a bit more about your great-great-grandfather. I was going to go to the Library to do some research. No one else really goes there, so the internet's really fast," Harriet said.

"I'll text Rafa," Gabi said.

She pulled out her iPhone, and typed:

"Hi Raf are u going straight home after school? I'm thinking I might stay and do some homework with Harriet"

A blue bubble appeared almost instantly under her message:

"No worries. I'll see u at home u happy to walk"

Gabi sent him a smiley emoji then wrote:

"Yep. See u at home tell UM I'll be back in time for dinner"

"I'm staying," she told Harriet.

They hurried back to Harriet's dorm where they got changed, then headed over to the library.

Unsurprisingly, it was empty.

Everyone else was probably making use of the free time between classes and dinner to watch Netflix in their rooms, or take part in after school sports.

The library was a five-sided building with large windows along four sides. The book shelves were arranged at right angles to the windows so they allowed as much light in as possible. This meant the library was very bright and airy.

There were study tables set out in rows in the centre of the library and this is where they both sat, next to each other.

Harriet took out her laptop and, once she had connected to the Wi-Fi, went straight to Google, typing:

"Ravi Dos Santos"

She hit search and a number of results came up, but nothing of any value. There were lots of "dos Santos" on Facebook, Instagram, and on all the other social media sites.

Loads of "Ravis" too.

She tried everything:

"Ravi dos Santos headteacher"

"Ravi dos Santos Scientist"

"Ravi dos Santos teacher"

"Ravi dos Santos Capel Cross"

"Ravi dos Santos King Edwards School"

None of these searches found anything of any use.

She started typing "Ravi Dos Santos" one last time and as she did Google made a suggestion they hadn't considered:

"Ravi Dos Santos alchemist"

There at the top, among the usual mix of Social Media profiles was a single website:

www.alchemyatoz.com

The subtitle read: *A complete list of alchemists and their achievements through the ages.*

Harriet clicked on the link.

CHAPTER FIVE

The website opened. It was an old HTML based page, probably built in the mid to late nineties. Gabi remembered having seen a similar website when she had been shown the unchanged website for the movie Space Jam. To her it looked like a relic of days gone by. Her uncle would probably remember all websites looking like this.

The blocky text looked like it had been typed on a typewriter, which added to the page's retro feel.

Across the top of the page were the words:

ALCHEMISTS THROUGH THE AGES

Under that was a row of letters from A to Z, all underlined indicating they were links.

"Click on R" said Gabi.

Harriet clicked on the letter R and was taken to a page with a single entry:

Ravi Dos Santos - Alchemist 1693 - 1787

"Wow!" Harriet exclaimed, "He was almost a hundred years old when he died! That almost never happened back then."

"Read what it says," Gabi said.

Harriet scrolled down a little and started reading:

Ravi Dos Santos was 27 years old when he came to the UK. He arrived as a stowaway on a ship from South America. No one knows who his parents were. Unlike other alchemists who seemed content in trying to find the secret to turning base metals into gold, he dedicated his life to trying to uncover the secret powers hidden within gemstones. His scientific studies allowed him to become a well-respected educator and by the time he was 39 years old he appeared to have stopped publishing any of his research into the power of gemstones. After his death in a fire in 1787 his journal was discovered in a safe hidden inside the wall of his classroom. Much of the journal was filled with indecipherable scribblings but what could be read was published a few years later in 1795. The book was given the title An Alchemist's Journal by R.D.S. His name was never mentioned in the book and only 10 copies were printed and bound as more of a novelty piece. The copies were paid for by a Mr M. Contritum. One was gifted to the school at which he taught. The others have been lost.

Not much else is known about this man's life, but he is of note as he is mentioned in the work of other alchemists and seemed respected in his field of gemstone studies.

"Is that all it says?" Gabi asked.

Harriet scrolled and clicked "next" but that simply took her to another page with another alchemist's details.

"Looks like it," she said, "But I wonder what happened to his book."

Jumping up from her chair, Gabi ran over to the

computer terminal that kept a record of all the books in the library: "If they've got it, it must be recorded somewhere."

She logged in using her school account number and listed the books by author.

There were thousands of books listed. She scrolled to S for Santos but there was nothing shown under that name.

She tried R for Ravi but again had no joy. She even tried D for Dos Santos but nothing seemed to be listed under any of those names.

Harriet said: "What if they don't know who wrote it?"

Gabi searched for "unknown authors" and found several entries. She scrolled through them all until she came across an entry that appeared to be exactly what she was looking for:

"Alchemist's Journey - Unknown Author. Curiosity Book. Section Z8."

They almost ran across the library to get to section Z8, but to their disappointment the numbering system stopped at Z6.

"I don't get it," Gabi said "why is it not here?"

At this point one of the teaching assistants, Mr Morvay, walked into the library. He can't have been more than twenty-one or twenty-two years old. He often helped out in the library as he was finishing his degree to become an English teacher in his home country of Hungary.

"Are you girls ok? Need any help?" He asked, almost shouting across the room.

"We're fine," said Harriet.

"Actually," Gabi said, shooting a sideways glance at her friend, "we're looking for a book that's meant to be in Z8 but we can't find that section."

"Ah, yes," Mr Morvay said, "I was told to clear that section a couple of months ago. Z7 and Z8 were put into storage because no one was reading them. They're all the books that are more than one hundred years old. I put them all in boxes in the storage room. I think they're going to throw them in the bin."

Gabi's stomach tightened and a feeling of panic started rising. She had to see that book.

"Where are they? Please can we see them? I need to see this book!" she pleaded.

"Is it for a school project?" the teacher asked.

"Yes," said Harriet lying, "and we need to finish it today."

"OK," he replied, taking a bunch of keys from his pocket, "but don't tell anyone. Come with me."

He walked out of the main library, turned left, taking them past the junior reading library where all the fiction books were kept. He stopped by a door at the end of the corridor, unlocked it, and went in.

"It should be in a box marked Z8. It's in here somewhere…" he said, his voice trailing off as he looked at the piles of boxes, "But don't take too long. I need to go make a phone call but I'll come back to lock up in half an hour."

Mr Morvay walked away as Gabi and Harriet went into the store room. The room was about 3 metres wide and 5 metres long and was stacked high with boxes on either side.

They pulled boxes out, turning them one by one until finally Harriet exclaimed: "I think I've got it!"

She was standing by a box labeled "Z8 - Old books for destruction".

Harriet ripped off the tape that was holding the box closed and there, at the very top, was the book they had been looking for.

It was very old. The brown leather cover was tatty and worn. The gold embossed lettering on the front was barely legible, but they could both make out the words "Alchemist's Journal" and the initials "R.D.S."

Gabi opened the book carefully as the pages were yellow and crisp with age.

On the first page she read the title, then turned the page to the dedication. As she did, her blood ran cold.

It read:

> *To whoever finds this:*
> *Read with care.*
> *The world is more dangerous*
> *than you have ever imagined.*

CHAPTER SIX

"I'm not sure we should read this," Gabi said, "It's too creepy. This warning is exactly what that homeless guy said. It's freaking me out a bit."

"It's just a coincidence, "Harriet reassured her, "and anyway, surely it's easier to 'be careful' if we know what the author is talking about…"

"You're probably right." Gabi closed the book and they returned to the main library where there was better light.

Sitting at one of the study tables in the centre of the room, Gabi put the book down between the two of them and opened it to the introduction:

Introduction

Dear Reader,

This book is unique. It is comprised of a collection of journal entries written by an accomplished scientist and alchemist named Ravi Dos Santos. Unfortunately, the original journal, from whence these entries were taken, was severely damaged so some entries have been lost. Other entries were simply illegible or indecipherable, so these have been omitted.

Ravi's work was markedly different to many alchemists of his time. Unlike others, he was not preoccupied with the banal search for riches, the trivial pursuit of gold from nothing, and an eternal life in which to spend it. Ravi seemed focused on harnessing the power found in the very core of the earth, and appeared to believe there was spiritual power hidden within precious stones.

I had the honour and privilege of meeting him once, near to the school where he taught for many years, and at which he eventually died.

He was warm, affable, and was happy to talk to me.

Instinctively he seemed to know me. He empathised with the struggles I have been through and understood the path I have chosen, for he too had chosen a divine mandate - a spiritual mission.

We talked for many hours that day and developed an almost instant kinship and while we talked he revealed what he was working so hard to achieve.

I promised him I would help him share his work with the world.

It is with a deep sadness I must confess I never saw him again.

He died a few short months later and, when I was able to gain access to this, his last journal, I transcribed what I could to share with you now. Regretfully this book can only tell you the last few months of his life as his other journals have been lost or perhaps, I suspect, stolen.

I can only afford to print a few copies, so I pray a copy finds its way into the right person's hands. I hope and pray that person is you, dear reader.

Now read this book with care, for the world is more dangerous than you have ever imagined, and there are forces out there intent on bringing about chaos and destruction.

Learn what you can from the words in this book, and use this knowledge for good.

I leave you now with the words of Ravi Dos Santos himself.

Yours in perpetuity,

MC

"Well," said Gabi, as she finished reading the introduction, "he seems quite intense…"

"It does make me want to read more though…" said Harriet.

Gabi turned the page and began reading.

Much of the journal was filled with detailed notes of experiments, rambling thoughts on theology, angels and demons, until finally, towards the end of the book, Gabi found this entry:

17ᵗʰ July 1786

The אוֹר gemstone is revealing itself to be more powerful than I thought possible. I have discovered I have the power to harness its qualities and can use it to repel shadows. If my inheritance had been purer, or if I had my mother's strength, maybe I would have the power to command it to my whim.

I am grateful to God for granting me the gift of this stone, but I wish He had bestowed me with the knowledge and grace to actually use this for good.

I worry my grand-daughter is concerned I might be becoming obsessed.

When I return from my travels I am hopeful to have a stronger grasp on the powers it possesses.

29ᵗʰ July 1786

I am currently sat on a ship out on the Atlantic Ocean. Storms have raged unabated for the last few days and I have struggled to regain my sea legs. Oh to be young again!

Much has happened since my last entry.

Having discovered what I suspect is the final location of חרב אש I boarded this ship, The Alma Perdida, and am headed to the port of Salvador in the North East of Brasil. The captain estimated the journey will take a few weeks, which should give me time to locate my source, find the cave he told me about in his letter, and still get back in time for next academic term. We must be about eight days from port now.

Some of the crew on this ship are not happy with my

presence here. I expressed concern for the welfare of their "cargo" and was told I should "know my place" and that "it is not uncommon for travellers to be lost at sea". I have since noticed my meal rations have been reduced and the crew no longer speak to me.

I imagine the remainder of my journey will involve little more than remaining in my cabin or attending the mess room for meals.

The צבא הצללים may have its claws in the hearts of some of these men.

"What's with all the weird code?" Harriet asked.

"I don't know," Gabi said, "I'm just skipping over it. Maybe he had to write in code to protect his work?"

They carried on reading:

1st August 1786

They broke in last night. I noticed some of the crew leave the mess room while I was eating. By the time I returned to my room everything had been turned upside down. All my possessions were strewn across the floor, my bed was on its side, and my drawers were pulled out. I am grateful I keep אור in its pendant around my neck as it is easier for me to keep its existence secret.

I carry my journal with me at all times so they weren't able to steal this either. I can't be certain whether they were looking for anything specific or whether this was just a senseless act of vengeance for sharing my views on their human cargo.

The sooner I am off this cursed ship the better. There should only be a week left now.

6th August 1786

I write this from my hiding place in this jolly boat. I am sequestered under the canvas cover, as the crew are baying for blood. Since my last entry I have been smuggling what little food I could down to the cargo hold. Last night the first mate saw me returning to my cabin and challenged me, asking where I had been.

I am old now and my brain is not as quick thinking as

it used to be and I could not think of an excuse for my presence there.

I returned to my cabin but later heard the crew talking about getting rid of me, and how my presence on the ship was bad for business, so I have hidden inside this jolly boat. I hope when we dock the day after tomorrow I will be able to make a run for it while the crew celebrate a successful voyage. I imagine they will be drinking more than enough rum to make my escape possible.

I'll escape the ship and find my contact who should be able to provide me with safe passage to the Caverna Dos Anjos.

8th August 1786

Safety at last. We docked yesterday evening. I heard the tortured voices of the cargo being unloaded and later heard the crew singing loudly as they went ashore. I took the opportunity to leave my hiding place and found my way onto the dock.

I was due to meet Father Guilherme, my contact at the entrance to the Basílica do Senhor do Bonfim which was some distance from the port. I was hoping he would wait for me.

As I was leaving the port I heard shouting as the crew left a local drinking hole. One of them shouted: "There he is. Get him!" They started running after me. Despite being 93 years old, most people tell me I looked no older than 65 - part of my family inheritance - the Dos Santos have always remained young beyond our years.

I ran from them as they stumbled after me. I had to duck down an alleyway, where I hid behind an empty barrel until the group of drunken sailors gave up and walked away.

I quietly left the docks under the cover of darkness and made my way to the Basílica where Father Guilherme was waiting for me.

I am grateful for his hospitality and the delicious meal of rice and black beans he served me. Tomorrow we head out to the Caverna Dos Anjos where I will hopefully find what I've been looking for.

Gabi's phone pinged, pulling her out of the book, and she looked at the screen. It was a text message from Rafa.

She opened it and what she read made her completely forget Ravi's story:

"GET HOME QUICK! CAN'T TALK NOW"

CHAPTER SEVEN

The clock at the top of her mobile phone screen read 21:00.

She had completely lost track of time searching for, and then reading, the journal. She'd missed dinner and had forgotten to text her uncle and aunt to let them know.

There was something about the urgency of Rafa's text message which made her realise that was the least of her worries.

She thrust the book into Harriet's hands and said: "I've got to go. I'll text you."

She ran out of the library, turning left on the path that led towards the school chapel. It was starting to get dark and the clouds that covered the sky meant soon there would be no light other than the street lamps.

She ran around the chapel and out onto Brook Road, turning left to head back towards Capel Cross in the direction of home. The streets were fairly empty, although this wasn't unusual for this time of night, especially midweek, after all Capel Cross was not exactly a busy village. Most people were usually home by eight pm.

She ran past the local fish and chip shop where there were a couple of people buying their late evening dinners, but everywhere else was pretty much a ghost town. She ran past Tesco Express on the High Street where the usual group of teenagers was sat on the railings by the side of the road near the crossing. One of them shouted something at her, but she couldn't really make it out.

She finally turned off the main high street into a completely deserted residential area.

Gordon Road was a long wide road that ran parallel to Woodcroft Lane with large detached houses either side. There were street lamps but they were spaced further apart than in many other roads (something about the residents complaining the lights were keeping them awake at night) so the road was fairly dark.

That night the road was deathly silent. There was no music coming from any houses, no cars driving down the road, no one putting rubbish out in the bins. The shortest route home to Woodcroft Lane was via an alleyway that ran between the two roads. The alleyway was about halfway down Gordon Road. It was just a footpath, about five foot wide and was not very well lit at all. She rarely used it after dark, but she needed to get home quick.

She was about twenty metres away from the alleyway when she saw him; a figure on the pavement about fifty metres away, the other side of the entrance to the alleyway.

Walking towards her was a man wearing a long black coat that stretched down to his ankles, and torn, tatty jeans. He had grey hair and as the gap between them closed she could make out his "Faith No More" t-shirt. It was the same man from the train station.

It might have been a coincidence, Capel Cross is very small after all, but Gabi was taking no chances.

Picking up her pace she turned right into the alleyway. The man broke into a jog.

Gabi felt fear rising like a lump in her throat. She tried to push down the panic but this only seemed to make it worse. She was almost at full sprint when she turned to look back down the alleyway. He was right behind her, running at full speed, his black coat billowing behind him.

As she ran it was as though the darkness was pressing in either side of her, as though the fences that lined the alleyway were somehow getting closer. Panic threatened to overtake her as she heard the stranger's footsteps echoing behind her.

After what seemed like an eternity she reached the end of the cut-through and broke out into the open road of Woodcroft Lane. She turned left and saw her house.

It was completely ablaze. There were flames reaching high into the sky, lapping around the edges of the roof and bursting out of every window on every floor. Where the front door had stood when she left this morning there was just a dark void from which black smoke was pouring out.

She fell to her knees outside the house.

"Rafa!!!" she shouted, at the top of her lungs, "Uncle Mike! Auntie Em!"

Tears were streaming down her face as she turned to see if she was still being followed.

The man was nowhere to be seen.

She heard the sound of sirens in the distance and, although it felt like an age, less than a minute later the first fire engine came careening around the corner into Woodcroft Lane, lights flashing, as it sped up the road towards her.

The fire engines stopped outside her house and a firefighter with symbols on his shoulder came over and said: "Is there anyone inside?"

"I don't know," she replied, sobbing, "My Uncle and Aunt live there with me and my cousin, but I wasn't home when it started. I don't know where they are."

The chief firefighter turned away from her and barked orders at the rest of the team who were unrolling hosepipes from the pump.

She stood by, helpless as the firefighters fought the fire, dowsing the house with high powered jets of water. Police arrived a few minutes later and two officers got out of their car. They weren't the same two she had seen this morning, but that didn't really surprise her. It had definitely been more than long enough for a shift change.

The two officers went to speak to the fire fighters and, while Gabi couldn't hear their whole conversation over the noise, she heard the chief fire-fighter use the words "cause doubtful". He then pointed over to where Gabi was standing.

The officers walked over towards her.

The younger officer stopped in the road to make a call on his radio while the older police officer, a friendly looking man with greying hair and slightly unkempt eyebrows above his clear blue eyes, came over. Taking out his pocket notebook, he said:

"Hi, what's your name?" His voice was gentle and sounded kind, making Gabi feel a little calmer.

"G-Gabi," she replied, "Gabi Dos Santos."

With a slight nod of his head towards the fire, the police officer asked: "Is this your house?"

"Yes. Well it's my Uncle and Aunt's but I've lived with them since I was a baby, when they adopted me."

The officer scribbled some notes down in his notebook. "And when's your birthday?"

"7th July. I'm going to be seventeen in a few weeks." Gabi said.

"OK. Thank you," he said, putting his pocket notebook away, "My name's PC Blandford. I'm on the neighbourhood team down at Capel Cross Police Station. We don't know if there was anyone in there at the moment, so we're waiting to find out. I may have to take you to the police station in a bit to keep you safe and to make sure we can find out exactly what happened. OK?"

"OK…" she replied, "Can I try to call my uncle and aunt?"

"Of course," PC Blandford replied, "I'll be just over there if you need me."

With that PC Blandford walked across to the car where his colleague was standing and started talking to him.

Gabi pulled her phone from her pocket and dialled Uncle Mike's number. It went straight to voicemail. She tried Auntie Em. That, too, went straight to voicemail.

Finally, she tried Rafa's number. It rang and rang before she finally heard his voice:

"Hello, you're through to Rafa but I can't take your call right now. I must be doing something more important than talking to you. Please leave a message."

"Rafa, where are you? I'm outside the house. Call me back. Please call me back. I don't know what to do…"

As she took the phone away from her ear and pressed the red button to hang up, she heard a gruff voice whisper in her ear:

"I know what you should do," it said, "Run!"

CHAPTER EIGHT

Gabi froze. She didn't have to turn around to know exactly who the voice belonged to. Her breath caught in her throat as she could practically smell the man who had followed her home. She could feel his breath on the back of her neck as he whispered again: "Run, Gabi. Run!"

Everything in her told her to do what he said; to run and not look back, but she had also always been taught to go to the police if she were ever in trouble. And if ever she was in trouble, it was now.

Under her breath, and without looking back, Gabi whispered: "I'm not running."

She stepped off the pavement into the road and walked slowly towards the two police officers who were still stood by their car. "Officers?" she said, "That man's just threatened me."

She pointed to where she had been standing mere seconds before.

"What man?" said PC Blandford, "There's no one there."

Gabi turned to look and the colour drained from her face. He was right. There was no one there, just a few firefighters milling around and some neighbours standing at their front doors, watching as the only home she had ever known burned to the ground.

"I swear there was someone there," she said, trying to hold back tears, "he was right there…"

Her voice trailed off as the enormity of the situation slowly started to sink in. Her aunt and uncle might be dead. Rafa might be dead. Where would she live? Who did this? What would happen to her school work? All her childhood toys were in the house. Had they lost everything? Who was that man?

"Come," PC Blandford's kind voice cut through the myriad of thoughts swirling through her head, "Come to the police station with us. We need to take a statement from you. But, most importantly, we also need to make sure you're safe. If there is some weirdo out there following you then we need to make sure he can't get to you. Come on."

He placed his hand gently on her shoulder and guided her towards the back of the police car where he opened the door for her. "Don't forget your seatbelt," the officer said before closing the car door. She fastened her seatbelt and leant her head back against the headrest as the two police officers got in and the younger one started the engine.

"Was anyone home?" she asked quietly.

The two officers exchanged a glance, neither one appeared to want to answer the question. After a few seconds the younger officer said: "We don't know the full details at the moment, but it does look like there were at least two people in the house. We don't know who they are yet."

Gabi felt numb as silent tears rolled down her face.

No one spoke again until just after 11 PM when the car pulled into the police station.

PC Blandford opened the door to let Gabi out. "It's child locked," he said, trying in vain to lighten the mood a little, "we sometimes have to put prisoners in the back and don't want them to run away!"

Gabi didn't answer. She walked towards the small police station. It was just a Victorian detached residential house that had been converted into a police station. There were large bay windows either side of the entrance. It was made of red bricks and would have been a beautiful home at some point in the past. The windows were all double glazed, but it still looked a bit tatty on the outside.

When they walked in she noticed that, while the floor in the corridor was made of beautiful black and white tiles, the walls were all painted magnolia, a creamy off white that had yellowed with age. There were posters lining the walls with phone numbers for law firms, anti-domestic abuse campaigns, and something about a police federation. There were two doors on the right-hand side, just past the "front office", that had a picture of a man and a woman on them. At least she now knew where the toilets were.

PC Blandford led her into a room on the left. It was the kitchen. He said: "Grab a seat," indicating an old chair pulled up to the table, "I'll make you a cup of tea." With that he turned, filled the kettle, and switched it on.

Gabi sat, stunned by everything that had happened. Less than three hours ago she had happily been researching her however-many-greats-grandfather in the school library with her best friend, and now she was sat in a police station, her house burned down, her family missing, possibly dead.

"How d'you take your tea?" the officer asked.

"I don't know. However," Gabi replied. She didn't often drink tea.

He brought over two mugs of tea and sat on a chair across the table from her.

"Hey, listen, I know it's not easy going through this. I can't imagine what you must be feeling, but I need to take a statement from you. Is that ok?"

"I guess," she said "I haven't got much I can tell you really. I got a text from Rafa then came home to find it on fire."

"That's fine," he said, "we just need to clarify a few details and get everything written down officially. But I will need to get someone from Social Services to come in and make sure we do everything by the book. It's only because you're under eighteen so you need to have what we call an *appropriate adult*. "

"Are Social Services going to take me away? I don't want to go into some foster place. I won't know anyone. I just want to go home…" As she finished her sentence she was struck by the impossibility of that request. She had no home to go back to. She had nothing. She folded her arms on the table and rested her forehead on them, staring at the floor under the table as her tears fell again.

"Listen, I'll see what I can do," PC Blandford's kind voice sounded sincere, "I just need to go speak to my sergeant first and we'll work out what's best, ok? I'll leave you in peace for a few minutes while I do that, alright?"

He walked out the room, allowing the kitchen door to close behind him, and for the first time since the fire, Gabi was completely alone.

Sitting there in silence she listened to the sounds of the police station. She could hear a police radio somewhere in the distance, someone talking on the phone, and the sound of a toilet flushing.

Then she heard the backdoor open and two new voices.

"Hey Matt! Heard you went to a fire and you've had to take a child into Police Protection?" the first voice said.

"Sounds like a good job!" chimed in the second.

The familiar voice of PC Blandford said: "Yeah. It's a weird one. Looks like arson. Poor girl's lost her whole family. Firefighters found two bodies in the living room who we think are her aunt and uncle. They're still looking for her cousin. She's got no other relatives. Her parents died in a car crash when she was a baby. She's in the kitchen, so best not go in there. I'm just waiting for the Skipper to get off the phone so we can work out what we're doing with her."

Gabi's heart felt like it was trapped in a vice. She now

had confirmation. Her aunt and uncle were dead.

She pulled out her phone and tried to call Rafa again, but there was no reply. It went straight to voicemail again, and as reassuring as it was to hear his voice, Gabi found herself becoming angry. "Just pick up!" she shouted at the phone, crying, "Just bloody pick up! I can't do this on my own…"

When his voicemail kicked in again, she slammed the phone down on the table and let out an anguished cry. There was nothing she could do. She just wanted someone to hold her and tell her it was all going to be ok.

After about twenty minutes, PC Blandford hadn't come back. She could still hear muffled voices talking in the distance but they were too far away for her to hear what they were saying. She stood up and walked over to the kitchen door, cradling her cup of tea in her hands.

She was about to pull the kitchen door open when there was a sudden knock on the window. She spun around, dropping her cup of tea in shock.

Another knock.

It was dark outside and the windows were frosted. With the lights on in the kitchen she couldn't see anyone there. "Who is it?" she shouted.

There was no reply.

The muffled voices had stopped talking now and she could hear the sound of footsteps coming back towards the kitchen. She flung the window open, hoping to catch whoever was there, but instead, all she found was a folded piece of paper, shoved between the window and the window frame.

Unfolding it she read four handwritten words:

Trust no one

Run

She was staring at the note, written hurriedly on the crumpled piece of paper, the window still wide open, when PC Blandford burst in.

"Are you OK?" he asked.

"I think so…"

The lights flickered and suddenly the room was plunged into darkness. Gabi felt something cold pass through her body, like an icy gust of wind, and the lights came on again.

PC Blandford was standing right behind her. He appeared taller than he had seemed before. His shoulders were back and he suddenly didn't seem so gentle.

"What were you doing?" he shouted, "Were you trying to escape?"

"N-no" Gabi stammered, "the window - someone…"

Before she could finish what she was saying, he lunged at her, trying to grab her by the throat. His eyes were wild and were somehow darker than they had been earlier. Gabi didn't have time to think and simply reacted, striking the officer square in the middle of his chest with the palms of both hands. The officer flew backwards, both feet off the floor. He careened through the air, striking the fridge in the corner of the room, before slumping to the floor.

Gabi pulled the kitchen door open and ran into the corridor.

The young officer from earlier was standing at the men's toilet door to her left. Two officers she hadn't seen before were standing between her and the exit to the police car park. A man she presumed was the sergeant was standing to their left, blocking the staircase that led to the next floor.

The only option available was the female bathroom. Gabi ran across the corridor into the ladies' toilets and saw a window at the far end of the cubicles. Running to the window she grabbed hold of the handle just as she heard angry shouts from the corridor:

"Oi! Get back here!"

"Don't let her get away!"

"Nick her!"

To her surprise the window opened easily and she climbed out into the car park as the door burst open and the four officers piled into the bathroom.

Gabi did exactly what the note had told her to:

She ran.

She turned left out of the police station car park onto a road she didn't really know. Behind her she heard the angry voices of the police officers chasing her. She could see their torches in the poorly lit car park, their radios lighting up on their chests. She heard one of the cars start up and within seconds she saw the blue lights flashing on the reflections of the houses she was running past.

Then there was an almost imperceptible flash of light and silence.

She was alone.

Completely alone.

In a field she knew only too well:

Upper Deacon, by the Cricket Pavilion, at King Edward's School.

CHAPTER NINE

Gabi trudged slowly towards the dark shadowy shapes of the school's boarding houses. She had no idea how she had arrived at school, or why PC Blandford had suddenly tried to grab her by the throat. At that moment all she wanted was to see a friendly face.

Under a sea of stars, she made her way along the moonlit path that ran along the edge of Upper Deacon to Aragon House. She pulled her phone out of her pocket to call Harriet. It was on 1% battery. She dialled Harriet's number. *"Please answer. Please answer."*

It rang eight times before she heard a muffled "Hello?" and her phone died. At least Harriet was awake now.

She ran to the back of Aragon and picked up some small stones from the flower beds that ran along the back of the house. Harriet's room was on the second floor, second window in. Very carefully she threw a stone up at the window.

The first one missed. She had never been particularly good at sports. The second one, however, hit the window with a soft tap.

After a brief pause the light came on, the curtains moved aside, and Harriet appeared at the window, in her pyjamas. She opened the window. "What are you doing here?" she said.

"Shhhh," said Gabi, "can you let me in? I don't know what to do."

Harriet closed the curtains and a couple of minutes later the downstairs window to the prep room, where the juniors did their homework, opened and Gabi climbed through, careful not to make any noise.

They crept upstairs to Harriet's room and Gabi went in and sat on the edge of the bed. Harriet closed the door behind them and Gabi burst into tears. She was finally safe.

"They're gone," she sobbed, "they're all gone."

Harriet sat on the bed beside her. She put both her arms around Gabi and held her tight. Within moments Gabi's tears subsided and she gave in to sleep. Harriet covered her with a blanket and lay down on the floor, using her fresh towels for pillows and a dressing gown as a blanket. For her, sleep didn't come so fast. Her mind was racing.

At around 2 AM, the moon slipped behind a cloud and the room was plunged into darkness. Harriet finally fell into a deep sleep, her dreams plagued by questions, shadows, and flames.

Gabi woke at 7 AM when Harriet's phone alarm went off. It was playing "Re-arrange" by Biffy Clyro, Harriet's favourite band. It took her a few seconds to remember where she was. She lay there for a few minutes wondering whether maybe everything had just been a bad dream and that any moment now she'd wake up to the sound of Auntie Em's cheerful voice.

Instead she heard the sound of male voices in the corridor. They were getting closer. Men weren't allowed upstairs in the girls' boarding houses. Even male teachers weren't allowed up here. She heard one of the men saying: "I'm sorry, we need to find her. Unfortunately, she's a suspect in a very serious incident where one of our colleagues died. If her friend knows where she is then we need to speak to her."

Gabi rolled off the bed, landing on top of Harriet,

waking her up. "Harriet! Harriet!" Her words were a hushed whisper, but loud enough to wake her friend, "They can't find me. Tell them you've not seen me!"

The voices were getting closer, still talking about an incident at a police station where an officer had been stabbed. "Get under the bed," Harriet said, "I'll cover for you."

Gabi crawled under the bed and Harriet lay down on the mattress, pulling the duvet up to her chin just as there was a gentle tap on the door. Mrs Todd's voice said: "Harriet? Are you up?"

There was a pause.

Then the door burst open and Mrs Todd squeaked in surprise as two large, angry looking police officers pushed her aside and barged into the room.

"Have you seen Gabi Dos Santos?" the first one asked.

"No," Harriet started saying, "I've not - "

"Don't lie to us!" the second officer almost shouted, the tone of his voice was less than friendly, "We know she was here last night."

"She wasn't," Harriet said, "The last time I saw her was at the library yesterday evening when she took off suddenly. I've not seen her since. She hasn't even sent me a text message." That last part was true. "Do you want to see my phone to check?" she added, reaching for her phone.

The two officers looked at each other, then the first officer said: "No. It's fine. Just make sure you tell us as soon as you hear from her."

"Is she in trouble?" Harriet asked.

"We just need to make sure she's safe," the second officer said, "Nothing to worry about, but she's had some family issues last night and she's missing. We've been tasked with finding her. Any idea where she might go?"

"No idea," Harriet said, "She always hangs out with me or at home. Have you asked her cousin Rafa?"

"We don't know where he is either," the first officer

said.

"But we can't talk about that," the second officer gave his colleague a dirty glance, "Data Protection, you know. Let's go."

The officer took hold of his colleague's arm and pulled him out of the room. Mrs Todd mouthed the word "Sorry" to Harriet as she pulled the dorm door shut and followed the officers down the corridor.

Harriet knelt on her bed, watching out her window until she saw the two officers get into the police car that was parked outside. Once the car had driven away she said: "They're gone. Now you have to tell me what's going on."

Gabi crawled out from under the bed and sat at Harriet's desk. She noticed the Alchemist's Journal was open on the desk. Harriet had clearly been reading it without her.

She told Harriet everything that had happened, from Rafa's text message, to being chased home, to the fire, to the police station, to getting back to school.

She finished her story saying: "The police are lying though. I heard them say I killed one of their colleagues. That's what they told Mrs Todd before they came in. It's why I hid."

"Why would they lie?" Harriet asked.

"I don't know," she answered, "but I need to get out of here."

Harriet stood up. She walked to her wardrobe and picked out a black hooded top, a white t-shirt and some clean jeans. "Put these on. They should fit."

Gabi did as she was told while Harriet got dressed, picked up a rucksack, and put her charger, her laptop, and The Alchemist's Journal in the main section. She did up the bag, slung it over her shoulder and said "Wait here," as she walked out the dorm.

Harriet pulled the door closed behind her. She was gone for what felt to Gabi like an age but then the door opened again and Harriet put her head in the room, whispering: "Come on. Everyone's at breakfast."

The two girls crept quickly along the corridor and down the stairs. They went out onto the path at the back of the boarding house, turned left and headed towards the main road.

As they approached Gurdon's Field they turned left again onto a footpath that led into the wooded area at the back of the school. They knew this was the path with the least chance of being seen by a teacher. They followed it along the edge of the field, away from the road, into the woods. Once under the cover of the trees they were able to slow their pace a little.

The path led them through the woods to an old wire fence that ran along the school boundary. They crawled under the fence where the ground had eroded a little and headed up a rabbit trail up to a road at the back of the school. Many pupils used this path at the weekend to get out of school without being seen. Couples would often leave the grounds to head to "The Valley" - a large field, in a valley, just the other side of the road, where they would be free to do those things couples do.

The two girls didn't see anyone that day, but knew if they turned left the road would lead them to the railway station where they'd be able to get away from Capel Cross.

They walked in silence along the quiet road.

After a few minutes Gabi suddenly grabbed Harriet's arm and whispered: "What's that noise?"

They both stopped to listen. There was a third set of footsteps that stopped just after they did.

As the girls started walking again, the other footsteps started too.

"I think someone's following us," Harriet said, "come on!"

They picked up their pace and rounded a corner, heading back towards Brook Road, the road that would lead them to the train station, and there, looking straight at them, no more than fifteen feet away was the stranger from the day before.

The two girls froze.

"Do you believe me now?" he said, "You really are in very grave danger."

On the road from school

CHAPTER TEN

For the third time in 24 hours, Gabi felt her chest tighten. She wanted to scream.

"Don't be afraid," the stranger said, "I'm not here to hurt you."

Gabi felt Harriet's hand gripping hers, tugging at her, trying to pull her away, but Gabi's feet seemed to be planted firmly to the spot.

In the distance she heard a siren wailing. Then another started up.

"There's isn't much time," the man said, "they're coming."

He reached out and took hold of Gabi's hand. He was gentle, like a father taking hold of his daughter's hand, yet his sense of urgency never diminished. She had no choice. She could take a chance with this stranger, or run back into the grip of the police who had already tried to kill her twice.

She released Harriet's hand and took a step towards the stranger. "Don't try anything," she whispered and turned to her friend, "Harriet, I don't think we've got a choice."

The stranger led her along the road a further twenty metres or so with a reluctant Harriet following behind. "I've got a car," he told them, "we need to get away from your school."

Parked in a layby was an old Ford Focus, the original shape from around the turn of the century. Rust had started to cause the paint around the wheel arches to bubble and peel away. There was green moss growing along the edges of the window trim, and the number plates were barely legible due to water damage. The stranger clicked a button on a key and the indicators flashed as the doors unlocked. "Central locking still works," he said, flashing a grin. Gabi didn't smile back.

Gabi and Harriet climbed into the back seat as the man sat down behind the steering wheel. He turned the engine on and the car started first time.

"Where are we going?" Harriet asked.

"We just need to get out of Capel Cross for now," he replied, "so we can get some distance between us and the police. We'll go to Guildford."

Guildford was a large county town about 20 minutes away from Capel Cross. It was busy enough, and both girls knew they would be less conspicuous there. The car pulled away from the layby and headed towards Brook Road.

They turned into Brook Road and drove past Queen Alexandra house, the junior boarding house where they had both started their secondary school lives. They went past the chapel, then turned left onto the main road that ran past the front of the school. "Get down!" the stranger said suddenly, "Get down!"

The two girls lay down towards the centre of the backseat so they would be below the window. A police car with flashing lights sped past them in the opposite direction. Gabi lifted her head slightly, just in time to see it turn right into Brook Road and disappear out of view.

The stranger drove at the speed limit through Capel Cross, careful not to draw attention to himself, before eventually reaching the motorway junction that led towards Guildford.

"You can sit up now," he said, as he put his foot

down, getting the car up to the national speed limit, "we'll be ok for now."

The two girls sat up. "Can we at least know your name?" Gabi said.

"Of course," he said, "My name's Melchiriel. My friends call me Melc. I'm a friend of your mother's."

Gabi felt the blood drain from her face: "You what?"

"Let's get to Guildford. I'll explain everything when we're safe."

They drove in silence for about 15 minutes. Gabi allowed herself to just stare out the window, her gaze fixed on nothing in particular. She watched as the central reservation barrier became a solid grey blur in the centre of her vision, her mind filled with questions.

Melchiriel pulled off the motorway and drove into a residential area before driving up a hill and parking in the car park outside Guildford Cathedral.

"We'll be safe in here," he said, "plus, their café does a great breakfast…"

Melchiriel locked the beat-up Focus as they walked away from it and headed towards the large entrance doors of the red brick cathedral. This cathedral was different to others Gabi had seen. This one wasn't covered in gargoyles, or ancient carvings of the Green Man, or saints of centuries ago. It was modern, made of what looked like expensive house bricks, with double-glazed glass doors.

As they walked in, she marveled at the size of the cathedral's interior. Light grey stone pillars stretched high towards the ceiling, while hundreds of simple wooden chairs lined the stone floor. There was an aisle down the middle, at the end of which, far in the distance, was the altar, adorned with a green cloth and a simple silver cross.

Melchiriel didn't slow down. He headed straight to the Season's Café, which was deserted except for one old man sat at a table in the corner reading a Bible.

"What do you want to eat?" Melchiriel asked, "It's on me."

Gabi realised how hungry she really was and said: "Can I get a Full English?"

"Great choice! That's what I'm having," Melchiriel said. He seemed to be starting to relax; "How about you Harriet?"

"Same, please," she said quietly.

Melchiriel ordered the food from a smiley middle-aged lady with bright blue eyes, and was handed an empty milk bottle with a numbered wooden spoon in it. Gabi thought this was a little superfluous as there really was only one other person in the café. Nevertheless, Melchiriel took the bottle and placed it at the end of their table as they sat down. He had selected a table at the opposite end to the old man, and sat where he could see the door.

"Good," he said, appearing to aim the comment at no one in particular, "good… they can't get to us in here."

"Who can't get to us?" Harriet asked, "The police?"

"No, no. The Army of Shadows," he replied.

"The what?" said Gabi.

"The Army of Shadows," he repeated, "It doesn't surprise me you've not heard of them. But they can't get to us in here."

"Listen, Melc," Gabi said, "there's nothing to stop me from telling the lady at the counter that you've kidnapped us, she'll call the police, and you'll get arrested, so you better tell us what we're doing here, how you know my mum, and why we should trust you."

"You're right," he said, "That's fair. I'll start at the beginning…"

CHAPTER ELEVEN

"First off, I want you to know I'm sorry I scared you," Melchiriel started, "I just needed to keep you safe. It was the last thing I promised your mother."

Gabi was silent. She sat across the table, facing this strange man. The same strange man who had begged her for spare change. The same strange man who had chased her to her house when it was burning down.

"Wha-What do you know about my mother?" she asked, her fear subsiding a little.

"She was just like you," he replied, "and she was my friend."

"I was only one when she died, I've got no way of knowing if you're telling the truth."

Melchiriel pulled an old leather-bound book out from his inside coat pocket. He opened the book, reached inside the front cover, and took out an old photograph. The photo was creased and crumpled around the edges. He placed it on the table and said "Take a look."

Gabi reached across and picked up the photograph. Under the halogen spotlights of the café she could see her father and her mother on their wedding day. Her mother was resplendent in her simple white dress and her father was beaming. They looked so happy. She felt a sudden pang of sadness at the thought that she never got to know them. She had no memory of their voices, their laughter, or how their hands felt holding hers. She noticed her mother's necklace; the same one she was now wearing herself.

In the photograph, next to her mother was Melchiriel. The t-shirt was gone, replaced instead with a black shirt, unbuttoned at the collar. His jeans weren't ripped in the photo, but he was still wearing the same long leather coat. He didn't look like he had aged a single day since.

"That was taken just over eighteen years ago," he said, "your parents were so happy."

"I've got so many questions… How did you know them?" Gabi asked.

"I'll get to that," Melchiriel said, "but first…"

The lady from behind the counter interrupted the conversation as she delivered their food. A full English Breakfast had never looked so delicious. Gabi and Harriet picked up their knives and forks and started digging into the big plates of sausages, bacon, fried eggs, cooked tomatoes, hash browns, fried bread, and toast. Gabi pushed her black pudding to one side. She had never understood how people could enjoy eating something made almost entirely of pig's blood.

Melchiriel spoke again, his voice hushed: "Have you heard of the Nephilim?"

Gabi shook her head.

"Aren't they a heavy metal band?" Harriet asked, "I think my dad has a CD of theirs."

Melchiriel smiled. "Yep. Fields of the Nephilim. I'd forgotten about them. Not my cup of tea if I'm honest. That's not what I'm talking about though."

He picked up the leather-bound book from which he had taken the photograph and flipped it open to a page near the start. Gabi recognised the way the text was laid out. Two columns per page, small writing with a big number at the start of each chapter. It was a Bible.

Melchiriel began reading: "Now it came to

pass, when men began to multiply on the face of the earth, and daughters were born to them, that the sons of God saw the daughters of men, that they were beautiful; and they took wives for themselves of all whom they chose."

He paused.

"*Sons of God* is an old-fashioned name for angels," he explained.

"I've never read that," Gabi said, "are you telling us the Bible says angels came and married humans?"

"Not marry," he replied, "but definitely slept with them."

"This has literally nothing to do with anything. Can't you just explain why you're here and how you knew my parents?"

"Patience," Melchiriel snapped. His eyes flashed with what could have been anger; "Let me continue."

He picked up his book again: "There were giants on the earth in those days, and also afterward, when the sons of God came in to the daughters of men and they bore children to them. Those were the mighty men who were of old, men of renown."

"I'm struggling to understand," Harriet said, "your Bible's really old."

Melchiriel closed his Bible and stood up. He turned and walked over to the table where the old man was still reading his Bible. He whispered something in his ear and the old man closed his book and handed it to Melchiriel.

He walked back to where they were sat and, opening the Bible up, flicked to a page near the start. He stopped at the end of the table and read: "In those days, and for some time after, giant Nephilim lived on the earth, for whenever the sons of God had intercourse with women, they gave birth to children who became the heroes and famous warriors of ancient times. Is that easier to understand?"

The two girls nodded and Melchiriel returned the old man's Bible. The old man waved at the two girls and called across the café saying: "It's great to see young people studying the Bible. Well done ladies." Gabi raised a hand in an awkward wave and looked back down at her food, not wanting to look like she was staring, despite his incredible, piercing brown eyes.

Melchiriel continued: "Thousands of years ago, angels and humans had children. They were called the Nephilim and the Bible tells their stories. Like it says, they became the heroes of the time. Some were good, some were bad, but they were all bigger, stronger, and wiser than other humans."

He paused to take a sip of the coffee he had ordered.

"Every hero in the Bible was descended from the Nephilim," he said, "David, who killed Goliath? Nephilim. Goliath the giant himself? Nephilim. Samson, the strongest man ever to have lived? Nephilim. King Solomon, the wisest king in history? Nephilim."

"But they're all men," Harriet said.

"That's only because of the way men have stolen history and made it their own," Melchiriel replied, "The strongest Nephilim have always been women, as the Nephilim gene is only passed down the female side. Have you heard of Jael?"

They both shook their heads.

"Jael was descended from the Nephilim. She drove a tent pole through a man's head. This led to a phenomenal victory for the Israelites. Deborah, the Judge in charge of Israel at the time? Nephilim. And the line continues throughout history - the prostitute who helped the spies in Canaan, Ruth, Elizabeth, who was Mary's cousin and mother of John the Baptist, even Mary herself."

"But are the Nephilim mentioned anywhere else?" Gabi asked, "I still don't understand what any of this has to do with my parents."

"Only twice," he replied, "once in the book of Numbers when Joshua's men find the city of Canaan, and once in Ezekiel, where he talks of an army of fallen

Nephilim, but after that the references slowly die out."

"Why?" asked Gabi.

"Well, like I said, the Nephilim gene is only passed down the female line, so even all the great male heroes could not pass on that divine strength and power to their children so, slowly, as humanity grew in number, the genes that made the Nephilim were all but lost. This is why I'm here, Gabi. This is why I came to find you. To protect you. You see, Gabi, you are the last of the Nephilim."

CHAPTER TWELVE

Rafa opened his eyes. Every part of his body ached. He felt as if he'd been run over. It was dark so he couldn't see the bruises that covered his face, neck, chest, arms, and legs. The room he was in smelt musty. Damp paper and old air.

Trying to move his arms he realised they were bound behind his back, tied to his feet. He was lying on his left-hand side on the floor. As his eyes adjusted to the dark he could just about make out some old chairs piled high against the stone wall. High above him he could see the outline of a narrow window. There was almost no light coming through, as the glass had been painted black, but there was just enough to let him know it was daytime.

He shuffled his body around, trying to work out where he was. He was clearly in an old store room of some sort. Along with the piles of broken chairs, there were some old metal shelves piled high with books, magazines, papers, old lamps, and all sorts of other junk. His body ached as he tried to move around. He wasn't able to roll over due to how he was tied, his feet pulled up to his hands behind him.

"Help!" he shouted, "HELP!"

"Silence."

The voice came from behind him. It was deep and resonant and something in it stopped him from shouting again. The voice had a distinctly British accent. "The Queen's English", he had heard it called. Each syllable was clipped, yet the words themselves seemed to roll off the tongue lazily, as if each word knew there was no hurry, after all, no one hurries royalty.

"I don't enjoy this sort of game," the voice continued, "I don't enjoy having to come to damp, dirty places like this. I find I am not at my most…" the voice paused as if looking for the word; "amenable?"

"Who are you? What do you want?" Rafa asked, "Let me go!"

"Quiet, boy. You may speak only when I ask you a direct question."

Rafa heard footsteps behind him, drawing closer. He turned his head as far as he could to try to catch a glimpse of the man to whom the voice belonged.

"Where is she?" the voice asked.

"Who? Where's who?" Rafa said, his voice barely more than a whisper. Fear was starting to take hold as he struggled to keep himself from panicking.

"Your sister. Where is your sister?" There was a note of impatience starting to come through.

"I don't have a sister," Rafa said, "you've clearly got the wrong person."

"Of course. My apologies. I misspoke," the voice continued, "Where is your cousin? Gabi is it?"

"Even if I knew I wouldn't tell you," Rafa replied, his voice a little stronger, a little bolder.

"Do NOT play games with me. Tell me where she is."

The room seemed to grow a little darker, as if light itself were afraid to creep through the spaces between the painted panes and the window frame.

Then a whisper in his ear as he felt hot breath on his neck: "Tell me where she is."

Rafa jerked his head to the right in time to see an enormous man standing over him. It was too dark to make out any features in this light, but the man's shoulders were broader than any he had ever seen. He could just make out his eyes in this light as they seemed to burn brightly, reflecting any light back out into the darkness. Shadows seemed to dance around him like the flames of a fire.

"I don't know," Rafa said.

"Does she know who she is?" the man replied.

"I don't know what you mean," Rafa said, trying to rest his head back down on the floor, "Let me go, I can try find her."

"Do you think I'm ignorant?" said the man, "Do you think I have not heard foolish attempts to foil me and fool me before? I am Damriel, Lord of the Army of Shadows. I am no fool, boy. You are never leaving this place. Your choice is simple. Tell me and die quickly. Lie to me and you will experience suffering the like of which you have never imagined. Trust me when I tell you, you do not want to feel the culmination of several millennia of my experience."

"I can tell you I don't want to feel the culmination of any more minutes of you talking…" Rafa said.

There was a pause.

"You have until tonight to reconsider your choice."

Damriel took a step back and spoke into the darkness: "Give him just a taste."

Suddenly the darkness was palpable. Rafa could feel it pressing against his skin, crawling up his arms and legs, spreading over his body, filling his eyes, his nose, his ears, his mouth.

Then came the pain. Excruciating pain. He could feel hot blades being pushed into the soles of his feet. His calves felt like they were being torn open, as if someone were ripping them apart with a hacksaw blade. His legs were suddenly forced together as invisible barbed wire was pulled tight around his thighs, his arms, and his neck, and all the air was pulled from his lungs. Trying to scream, it felt like he was drowning, as every breath he took seemed to empty his lungs.

His vision blurred and Rafa's world went black.
Then silent.

CHAPTER THIRTEEN

"The last Nephilim?" Gabi said, throwing down her knife and fork with a clatter; "Now I know you're full of crap. Harriet, come on, let's go."

She stood up to leave but Melchiriel reached across the table, putting his hand on her arm. "Wait," he said, "Please wait."

"No," she replied adamantly, "you've lured us here, told us some cock and bull story about me being descended from angels, and you want me to stay? You're a weirdo. A freak. You're probably a pervert."

Even as she said this she knew she was wrong. Something in his eyes made her words feel out of place. Out of line. His kind blue eyes were filling with tears.

"You know I'm not any of those things," he said quietly, "you *know* it."

He wasn't wrong. Something inside her told her there was some truth in what he was saying. At least in that last sentence. She pulled her chair out and sat back down.

"Can you prove what you're telling us?" she asked, "Or do we just have to believe you?"

Melchiriel visibly relaxed. With relief in his voice he said: "Who do your friends come to for counsel when they have a problem?"

"That's definitely you," Harriet said.

"Have you ever found yourself to be stronger than you thought?" Melchiriel continued.

"I don't think so…" Gabi said, before stopping as she remembered the police officer she had thrown across the room.

"Have you ever found yourself able to run faster than humanly possible, or travelling to places without knowing how you got there?" he went on.

"Only last night," Gabi admitted, "when I ran away from the police station I somehow ended up back at school, and I can't remember how I got there."

Melchiriel smiled and brought his hands together. "Yes! Yes!" he exclaimed, barely containing his happiness, "That's called Angelic Transportation. It's how angels can travel from one point on the globe to another. We tap into the spiritual realm and arrive where we need to be. It's incredible. Very few humans can do it. Only those who are true descendants of the Nephilim."

"I don't know how I did it though," Gabi said, "and I don't know that I could do it again."

"I can teach you," Melchiriel replied. "Now, - "

"Wait a minute!" Harriet interrupted, "You said *we*. You said '*We* tap into the spiritual realm'. What do you mean? I thought Gabi was the last Nephilim. Are you Nephilim too?"

Melchiriel let out a quiet laugh. "No, no. I'm not Nephilim."

"How do you know so much about it then? And how can you teach her?" Harriet continued.

"It's a long story," he said "and you're going to have to trust me on a lot of it. OK?"

They both nodded.

"I came into being over 5000 years ago. God himself crafted me the same way he crafted all my siblings. He took rays of pure light and lovingly shaped my face, my body, my wings. He called me into being and gave me my life. When I opened my eyes for the first time, all I could see was His face. That moment is seared into my heart. I remember it as vividly as I remember this moment we're in right now. I remember opening my mouth for the first time. I couldn't speak yet, but from my mouth flew songs of adoration that joined with thousands of my kin, worshiping the one true Ruler of All."

His eyes teared up as he spoke.

"Are you saying you're an angel?" Harriet asked.

"Yes. I was born an angel in the courts of the king. I was one of the heavenly choir."

"OK. Assuming we believe you," Gabi said curtly, "you don't look like an angel, and you definitely don't sound like you sing like an angel. Where are your wings?"

Sadness filled Melchiriel's eyes. "I'm getting there," he said.

"There were three others brought into being that day. I considered them my closest friends. You've heard of two of them. Gabriel, my brother, rose through the ranks and became the Archangel you have no doubt heard about. He delivered the message to Mary when Jesus was to be born. He spoke to Joseph in his dream and told him to go to Egypt. He is the head of the angelic army.

Lucifer, my other brother, you'll have heard of too."

"Satan?" Gabi exclaimed.

"Yes," Melchiriel continued, "He had the most beautiful voice you could ever hear. When he sang he could melt the very heart of God himself. Lucifer was often called to sing alone in the throne room, for his voice brought the King such pleasure. He eventually became the choirmaster, but more on him a bit later…" Melchiriel went quiet, staring off into the distance, lost in thought.

"You said there was someone else?" Gabi said, breaking the silence.

"Yes, sorry," Melchiriel continued, "Damriel, my best friend. He and I did everything together. We sang together, and could talk for aeons. We explored the universe, riding on waves of starlight and descending to the deepest depths of the sea. We saw so much, and it all brought us so much joy. We watched as Humanity came into existence. These beautiful, fragile beings, so like us, and yet so different. Every human seemed to be imbued with something we didn't have, and we couldn't put our finger on what that was. And God was fascinated too. More than fascinated. He loved humanity. Still does. He wanted humans to be everything we couldn't be. You see we loved the King but we had never known anything else. When there is only one option, it's not real freedom, not true love.

But humanity had choice. They had freedom. That's what they had that we didn't. They could choose who they loved. They could choose to love God, and they could choose not to. They could do good and they could do harm. We had never seen harm being done. It wasn't in our nature, and wasn't something we even considered because the choice simply wasn't there.

Lucifer was the first to fall. I remember watching in horror as he screamed at the King. He was jealous. For eternity his voice alone had been God's favourite thing. He was highly favoured. From among all the angels, he was the only one who could bring more light into the throne room with the sound of his song. He wore robes that reflected every colour of the rainbow, given to him by God himself.

Then humanity came along and suddenly he was no longer the King's obsession. I'm certain God still loved Lucifer, but His focus was on humanity. His focus was on these creatures, these creations, who were somehow lower than us, for they didn't have our power, yet also somehow higher than us because God appeared to care for them more.

Lucifer and I argued one day when he tried to convince me to leave. He told me he was heading to Earth to turn humanity against God so he could try to win back the King's affection. I told him his plan was stupid. I told him it's not how love works, but he wouldn't listen. He left that night, taking almost a third of all the angels with him. Together they infiltrated humanity, encouraging people to do things that would go against God's desire for peace, beauty, and serenity. Lucifer and his army wanted God to fall out of love with humanity.

There have been stories about Lucifer wanting to take control of Heaven. It's rubbish. He doesn't want to take control, he just wants to feel as loved as he did before. He's jealous. Nothing more.

He's still here, working in the background, still trying to turn humanity against God so that God would turn against humanity. He learned early on that he shouldn't be too obvious. Once humanity discovered his existence it actually caused many to turn back to God, repenting, turning away from *evil*, or *d'evil* - The Devil, as he became known."

"I've never heard it told that way..." Harriet said, "I've always been taught that the Devil just wants to hurt people and cause problems."

"It's not like that at all," Melchiriel answered, "He doesn't really care what happens to humanity, he just wants God to stop focusing on humans and return to the way things were before. So he works in the background, out of sight, out of mind, hoping that humanity will forget he exists. That way they'll have nothing to turn away from and will not return to God..."

He paused for a moment, then said: "Damriel's different. His story too is borne out of love, but the results have been far more devastating."

At the far end of the cathedral a choir started singing, the words of the Magnificat, the song of Mary. Their voices rose, filling every part of the giant building, echoing off walls and pillars, a perfect blend of melodies and harmonies - music in its purest form. Melchiriel stopped for a few moments and appeared to be just listening, lost in thought.

Eventually he continued his story: "After Lucifer fell there was a change in Heaven. Somehow the knowledge that leaving was an option meant remaining was a choice we each had to make. It was an easy choice for me. I had no quarrel with God. Believe it or not, I quite like rules. Or at least, I used to.

A decree came from the Throne Room that angels were not to visit Earth unless on direct instruction from God. We were to become messengers to humanity, communicating God's will to individuals as He required.

But some angels weren't content with following these rules. Some had fallen in love with the beauty of humanity and would leave through hidden portals, coming to Earth disguised as humans to spend time with humanity. Whenever we take on human form, our powers are diminished. We can still travel far and fast, and still have strength and wisdom, but we also feel pain, and hunger, and tiredness. But, as spiritual beings, it's the only way we can interact directly with the physical world.

There was always something exciting and incredible about feeling hunger that could be satisfied with one bite of an apple, or feeling tired and falling asleep on a soft bed, covered in a warm blanket. Oh, the joy of coming out of the bitter cold into a room warmed to perfection by an open fire. Nothing compares.

And so, many angels would sneak out regularly, temporarily giving up our powers to become part of humanity for a while. Damriel was one of them. He was gone more often than others, and this didn't go unnoticed.

Gabriel came to me one day and asked me about Damriel. He asked me if I knew where he was. He told me his presence was missed and that the King wanted to see him. He was concerned that Damriel might be hiding among the humans.

I then did something I had never done before. I lied. I told Gabriel I didn't know where he was. Somehow, I knew Gabe didn't believe me. He walked away saying 'Brother, I hope, for your sake, you're telling the truth.'

Damriel returned that night and came to see me. I told him what had happened and that I didn't think he should go back. I remember seeing sadness in his eyes, but he quickly became angry, shouting 'He can't stop me from going back. Who does He think He is? He can't stop me from seeing her!' Then he stormed out. It was the last time I spoke to him.

You see, Damriel had fallen in love with a human woman. Her name was Abital and she had dark hair, olive skin and bright green eyes. And she was carrying his baby. He wasn't the only one to have fallen in love with a human. Hundreds and hundreds of angels had taken on human form and had fallen in love. Some with men, some with women, all forbidden.

Gabriel was given the task of rounding them up and bringing them home. This became known as the Second Fall. In the thirty years that followed, many angels died, preferring to fight against Gabriel and his army, than leave their lovers and return to Heaven.

During this time, Damriel, who had always been a natural leader, rallied the Fallen to join him in battle against Gabriel. His son, Abdiel joined him in the fight. Together this rebel army ambushed Gabriel while he was out searching for them one night. He managed to fight them off, killing Abdiel while many of the others fled in fear but not before Damriel was able to seriously injure him, preventing him from returning to his angelic form.

This is where your story begins, Gabi."

Melchiriel looked her in the eyes, then continued: "Gabriel took refuge in an inn nearby. He remained there for two nights while he healed. On the second morning he was strong enough to return to Heaven. Nine months later the inn keeper had a baby. The baby was named Arella. And you are her descendant. And you are *his* descendant. You are the last descendant of the 'great' archangel Gabriel."

Gabi sat in silence while he gave her time for this to sink in. None of this made sense. The Bible wasn't real. Clearly these were just the ramblings of a mad man.

Shaking her head, she pressed her palms against the edge of the table and pushed herself back in her chair. "No," she whispered, "it doesn't make sense. None of it makes any sense."

"I know it's hard to believe. Your mother didn't believe me when I told her either."

"She knew?" Gabi didn't know how many more revelations she could take.

"Yes," his voice was heavy; "It's why Damriel killed her."

"She died in an accident. It was a car crash!" Gabi's voice was louder and angrier than she had expected it to be, "It was an accident."

"If only that were true," Melchiriel said, shaking his head, "It wouldn't bring them back but it would be less of a tragedy."

"Why? Why did he do it?" she asked, tears starting to flow.

"Damriel is very powerful. He can't be killed by normal means. There is only one way to kill an angel, whether they are good or bad: the sword of flames."

"The one from the story of the garden of Eden?" Harriet asked, breaking the silence she had held for a while.

"That's the one. When Lucifer first started turning humanity away from God, God put two humans in a beautiful garden and showed them what life could be like. God wanted them to see how good things could be, hoping they would choose to go out and make the whole Earth look like this perfect garden where there was no hunger, no anger, no thirst, no jealousy.

But Lucifer got in. He got to them and they chose to leave. So God put an angel, named Uriel, at the entrance to the Garden. Uriel was given a sword of flames with which to guard it. Uriel didn't need it to stop humans getting back in, but held it to stop other angels from entering.

When the Second Fall came, Uriel had already given up his post, for he too had fallen in love with a human. So Gabriel took the sword from him to protect himself and hunt down Damriel's army. When he was injured in battle he found an inn and sought help there. He knew he couldn't take the sword into the inn, so he hid it, knowing that only an angel would be powerful enough to wield it. But, when he returned to collect it, it was gone."

"Where is it now?" asked Harriet, sitting forward in her seat.

"No one knows for certain," Melchiriel said, "throughout history there have been rumours of swords that may have been the Sword of Flames, but no one can be one hundred percent certain."

"Like Excalibur?"

"Exactly right. Excalibur may well have been the Sword of Flames, but Arthur would not have been able to use it to its full potential. Other examples would include Mmaagha Kamalu, which is said to have glowed red when evil people are nearby. The Book of Mormon talks about the Sword of Laban which was used by Nephi to kill Laban and was then used as a model for other swords he made. In Cambodia there was talk of a sword that bestowed its owner with guaranteed victory - it was called Phra Saeng Khan Chaiyasi, or the Sword of Victory. But it's been lost for a good few centuries now."

Impatient, Gabi said: "What's all of this got to do with me?"

"Only a Nephilim is able to wield the sword to its full potential, for Nephilim carry the DNA of angels and, being human, also carry the breath of God, something we angels do not have, for while we were formed of light, it was God's breath that brought you to life."

"And that's why my parents died?"

"Yes. Protecting your family has been both my

blessing and my curse throughout history. I have sometimes been beloved, sometimes hated, but have always failed. You're my last chance."

"What happened?"

"Well, your mother knew she was being followed. She'd phoned me that Sunday afternoon and told me she needed to speak to me. We arranged to meet at a Little Chef on the A3 just down the road from here. I told her to bring you and to make sure your dad came too. She put the phone down and told me she was leaving and that's when -"

"Excuse me?" a voice said from just behind them. It was the old man from across the café, whose Bible Melchiriel had borrowed. He was standing right by their table. "Are you driving a really old Ford Focus?"

"Yes…" said Melchiriel, "Why?"

"I just thought I should let you know there's loads of police around it. I think they're giving you a parking ticket…"

Guildford Cathedral

CHAPTER FOURTEEN

Melchiriel immediately stood up, looking pale. "We have to go," he said abruptly, "come with me."

He pushed his chair back, turned, and headed to the far end of the cathedral. The two girls followed. He was not hanging around. Gabi found herself almost breaking into a run to keep up.

There were a few people in the Cathedral now, mostly drawn in by the early morning choir practice. Gabi and Harriet followed Melchiriel through some blue iron bars into a side chapel.

Above the altar was a floating statue of Mary, carved out of wood. Melchiriel said: "This is the Lady Chapel, and if I remember rightly…" he walked around the back of the altar and crouched down out of sight.

Gabi and Harriet stepped around the altar to see him running his hands along the back of the wooden altar table until they heard a click. A panel became loose and Melchiriel slid it left, revealing a set of stone stairs leading down into the ground. "Climb in," he said, "I'll go and speak to the police to find out what's going on. If I'm not back in half an hour, I want you to follow the tunnel. It comes out at the bottom of Stag Hill, near the canal. Get yourselves somewhere safe and I'll call you as soon as I can."

Gabi found it strangely comforting that he actually had a mobile phone. Maybe he wasn't as strange as she'd originally thought. Melchiriel paused briefly to take her number before sliding the panel shut, trapping them both inside.

The air in the tunnel was dry and dusty, and Harriet used her phone torch to have a look around. There were old fashioned light bulbs along the walls, and old cabling linking them. It looked like something built in the 1940s or 1950s. It definitely wasn't that old. The walls were made of brick and Harriet only had to walk down eleven steps to get to the entrance of a tunnel that stretched off into the distance. Neither of them could find any sort of light switch.

After a few minutes, Harriet said: "I better turn my torch off to save my battery." They were both plunged into complete darkness. The panel at the top of the stairs must have been completely sealed as there was absolutely no light getting in.

Minutes dragged by until finally, twenty-five minutes later they heard a click and the panel slid open. Melchiriel's voice called down to them: "Stay there. I'm coming down."

They watched as he climbed into the passageway and slid the panel shut behind him. "We can't use my car anymore. We'll have to go through the tunnel…"

He squeezed past the two girls and walked a few metres into the tunnel ahead of them. Harriet lit the light on her phone again and shone it towards him. Melchiriel was feeling around on the wall to his right. "It's around here somewhere…" he muttered to himself, "Ah, here it is!"

Suddenly the lightbulbs along the passage walls lit up, showing them just how long the tunnel really was. It stretched off into the distance as far as they could see until the lights abruptly seemed to stop.

"Come on," Melchiriel said as he started walking.

"What happened?" Gabi asked.

"There were police everywhere," he replied, "so I

asked them what had happened. I told them I was in charge of the cathedral carpark…" he chuckled at this, "No idea why they believed me! Anyhow, one of the young officers told me that an old Ford Focus had been seen leaving Capel Cross with two missing girls in it. Whoever told the police also got my number plate, so they know it was my car. They're probably going to watch it until the owner comes back.

I told them I had a clamp in my office so I could immobilise it for them if they wanted and they loved the idea so I got away and came here."

"Aren't they going to be looking for you as well now?" Harriet asked.

"Probably," he replied, "but hopefully I've bought us some time."

They walked on in silence for a while, the old lamps lighting their way.

"How long is this tunnel?" Gabi asked.

"It leads down to the river Wey, so it's about a mile and a bit. They built this just after the second world war when they wanted an escape route down to the river in case there was another war."

"What are we going to do when we get there?" Harriet asked.

"I'm not sure. We need to find somewhere safe where we can hide and work out what to do next."

Gabi stopped walking. "I think we need to get away from this area," she said, "but they're going to be looking for us wherever there's CCTV."

"Have you got an idea?" Melchiriel asked.

"Rafa has a car. It was definitely at home last night when the fire started. I bet it's still there. If we can get that we'll be able to drive somewhere away from the big towns and the CCTV. It might give us a bit of time to work out our next move."

"That's the wisdom of the angels," Melchiriel said, without any hint of irony, "we should be able to get the train back to Capel Cross from Guildford, and the river runs right past the station. It's risky, but if we can get back without being caught I think we'll be on the right track."

After what seemed like an eternity, they reached an old wooden door with large metal hinges. Melchiriel turned the handle and forced it open. Dust fell from around the edges as he allowed day light to flood the tunnel and they stepped out into the blinding sunshine.

CHAPTER FIFTEEN

Gabi stood blinking in the light for a few moments before she recognised the cinema building off to her right. "I guess it's this way," she said, turning right and heading back towards the city centre. Harriet and Melchiriel followed.

"Don't run," Melchiriel warned, "it'll draw too much attention."

Gabi slowed her pace a little hoping she looked more like someone who was a little late, rather than someone trying to run away from something. Within fifteen minutes they arrived at the station. The two girls waited by the doors while Melchiriel went to buy some tickets.

"Look!" Harriet whispered to Gabi, pointing at the headline on the local newspaper.

TWO TEENAGE GIRLS ABDUCTED FROM
PRESTIGIOUS PRIVATE SCHOOL

Under the headline was a photograph of the two of them together in their school uniform.

"We definitely need to get out of here," Gabi said, putting her hood up and hunching her shoulders a little to help hide her face.

Melchiriel returned with the tickets and, so they

wouldn't look like they were together, the three of them went through the platform barriers separately. They stood on the platform some distance apart waiting for the train that would take them the four stops back to Capel Cross. At this time of day there weren't many people catching the train toward Portsmouth. Everyone was either at work or at school, so there were only six other people on the platform.

The train arrived less than twenty minutes later and they boarded separate carriages before heading towards the centre of the train.

The third carriage was completely empty. Gabi chose a seat by the window and sat down, facing the direction the train was heading in. She'd never enjoyed travelling backwards, it felt like she couldn't see where she was going and it always made her feel a little travelsick.

Harriet joined her a few moments later and sat next to her.

Melchiriel sat down opposite. "It's about ten minutes from the train station to your house," he said, "I hope police aren't watching the station…"

The train pulled away and they sat in silence. There was something comforting about the clic-clac of the train on the tracks and, despite the fact she knew they were still in incredible danger, Gabi allowed herself to relax and feel safe, even if just for a moment.

The train stopped suddenly at Farncombe Train Station and Gabi opened her eyes. She couldn't even remember drifting off.

No one got on. She heard the guard's whistle and the train moved off.

Godalming Train Station was equally as deserted. With her head resting against the window she watched as one old man got off the train and an elderly woman greeted him with a smile and a hug. "Please mind the gap!" the Tannoy announced, and the train lurched forward again.

They were almost there.

As the train pulled out of Godalming and into the Surrey countryside, the door at the far end of their carriage slid open with a hiss as the train guard came in.

The guard was in his late forties. He was about five foot nine, and while he wasn't fat, he had quite broad shoulders and a little bit of middle age spread. His beard was a little unkempt, and his brown eyes looked tired. His greying hair looked a little like it needed a wash, but it was combed and as well presented as it had to be. Gabi thought he looked like someone who had just given up on trying to achieve anything more than getting through the day. "Tickets, please," he said, sounding bored. He had probably seen hundreds of tickets already today.

"Tickets," he mumbled again as he approached their seats.

Gabi pulled her hood down around her face as she reached into her pocket for her ticket. She didn't look up as she held it out to him.

The train rocked suddenly as it turned and went under the shadow of a bridge and daylight blinked.

It was all it took.

Something gripped Gabi's wrist. She looked up to see the guard holding her with his right hand, digging his nails into her skin. His bored eyes were now black, filled with a hatred she'd never seen before.

"Get off!" she shouted, trying to pull her hand back, but he was too strong.

"Nephilim," he growled, "my Master wants you."

Melchiriel rose to his feet. He seemed taller somehow. There was fire in his eyes.

"You cannot take her," he said. There was power in his voice.

The guard turned his head to look at Melchiriel.

"You," he said, "I've met you before."

"And I warned you then," Melchiriel replied.

Gabi didn't even see it coming. Melchiriel's right fist connected with the left side of the guard's face and he released her wrist, stumbling back.

Looking up slowly, the guard cradled his jaw, blood forming on his lips.

"I'm stronger than I was last time," he said, and threw himself at Melchiriel, both arms outstretched in front of him, his fists clenched. He appeared to have the use of invisible wings as his body flew through the air, connecting with Melchiriel's chest, causing him to be thrown back towards the other end of the narrow train carriage.

The guard landed on top of Melchiriel and punched him in the head, over and over again. Melchiriel's arms were powerless against the volley of blows the train guard was landing.

Harriet had slid from her chair and was hiding in the row of chairs behind. Gabi watched in horror as the guard put his hands on Melchiriel's seemingly lifeless neck and started squeezing.

"Let him go!" her voice sounded strangled, weak, "Let him go!"

"Oh I will, little one," the guard hissed, "I will. But. You're next."

He turned back to Melchiriel and lowered his head towards his neck: "Say goodbye, *Brother.*"

The guard opened his mouth to bite and before Gabi knew what she was doing she found herself putting her hands on the guard's shoulders. She grabbed hold of his shirt with two hands and pulled.

This time the guard really flew. He was thrown back, releasing Melchiriel and landing on his back in the middle of the carriage. Gabi felt a surge of power rush through her body as she launched herself at the guard, punching him hard in the side of his jaw. He stopped moving, then his body convulsed and Gabi watched as a shadow seemed to slide from his mouth, nose and eyes, then glide silently under the carriage door.

The guard remained motionless on the floor. He was out cold.

"What do we do now?" Harriet said. There was no concealing the panic in her voice.

"I don't know," Gabi replied. She felt strangely calm.

"We need to hide him," Melchiriel said, standing to his feet, rubbing his injured jaw. "Ouch," he added, "that hurt."

Between them they dragged the guard into the train toilet and closed the door. "He won't wake up for a while," Melchiriel said.

"What *was* that?" Harriet asked quietly.

"That's what they do," Melchiriel replied, "They can't move things in the physical realm, unless they're controlling a human. They can either convince a human to do something, but this takes a long time, or they can subvert a person and take over their whole body. That's what happened there. A demon took control of the train guard, probably when we went under the bridge. That's why he suddenly attacked us."

The train lurched as it slowed to a stop.

"Come on," Melchiriel said, "we're getting off here."

There were no police watching the train station. No one expected them to come back to Capel Cross of their own accord.

They alighted the train and headed for the village.

A short time later, in the train toilet, the guard found himself lying on the floor, his head pounding, his ticket machine broken. His knuckles were cut and bruised and he had no recollection of how he ended up there.

He sat very still for a moment then chuckled to himself.

It made a change from punching tickets.

Capel Cross Train Station

CHAPTER SIXTEEN

They walked through the streets of Capel Cross, all of them grateful that Gabi had grown up there so she knew the town like the back of her hand. They stuck to back roads and alleyways, avoiding any areas where there may be people. It only took them quarter of an hour to get back to Woodcroft Lane.

As they turned into the road, Gabi saw all that remained of her childhood home: a burnt, twisted shell of what had once been. Running through her head were the painful memories of happy times with her uncle and aunt, the silly squabbles with Rafa, and all the times he'd made her laugh.

She stopped. She was struggling to keep herself together and realised she had been running on adrenaline for the last few hours. A tear ran down her cheek and she felt Harriet's arm around her shoulder.

"Not yet, Gabi," she said, "I know it must hurt, but we need you to hold on just a little bit longer. As soon as we're out of here…"

Gabi wiped her eyes: "I know. I just hadn't really thought about what happened until just now. I'll be ok. Let's get Rafa's car."

There was blue police tape all around the outside of the house, and a squad car parked on the road. It was facing away from where they were but Gabi could see someone sat in the front seat. It didn't look like there was anyone else around.

"We're going to have to creep in around the back if we want to get to the garage without being seen," Gabi said.

Sticking to the very edge of the pavement, right up against the hedges, they crept along the road before ducking down a narrow alleyway that led to the back of the houses. Like many houses of that age there was a footpath that ran along the back of the row of houses, with gates into each garden.

Melchiriel went ahead and peeked around the corner into the footpath. "It's clear," he said, "they're not covering the back. Thank goodness for government cuts!"

They followed him up the path until Gabi whispered: "It's this one," indicating a gate on their left. She carefully turned the handle which opened without a sound. The gate swung open smoothly and quietly.

The garden was long and thin. The back of the house was about twenty metres away. To the right of the house was the garage, which seemed not to have been affected by the fire. Gabi had always loved this end of the garden, where plants had been allowed to grow a little bit wild between the trees. As a little girl she had called it "The Jungle", even though it was only a little overgrown.

She took a step forward and saw it. There on the floor in front of her was an iPhone. It was face down, the Spider-man logo on the back of its black case clearly visible. "That's Rafa's phone," she whispered as she bent down to pick it up, "he never goes anywhere without it."

"It looks like there was some sort of scuffle down here," Melchiriel said, pointing at some flattened bushes and broken twigs.

"That means Rafa's still alive!" Gabi exclaimed, "Maybe he's in the house!"

She turned, clutching the phone in her hand and started running towards the burnt building. Melchiriel lunged for her, trying to grab her and, in a hushed voice, said "Wait!" but it was too late. Gabi burst out of the undergrowth straight into the arms of a police officer.

"What have we got here?" the policeman said, taking hold of her wrist, "You shouldn't be here. It's a crime scene… wait a minute… Is your name Gabi?"

"I don't think I have to tell you…" her voice was trembling, instantly regretting her impulsive action.

"Oh, I think you do," the police officer said, reaching for his baton, his eyes turning dark. She'd seen the same look in the train guard's eyes, only minutes earlier.

A sudden thump, the sound of something landing on the ground six metres or so to Gabi's right, made them both turn to see a large branch on the grass. As they did Melchiriel seemed to fly from the bushes, grabbing the police officer around the throat and pulling him to the ground in a headlock. The police officer released Gabi's wrist as he fell to the floor. Melchiriel held a stick up to the man's throat, pushing the pointed end into his skin.

"Demon," he whispered, "don't move. You know what happens if I kill the host while you're inside him…"

"Ok, ok," the police officer was whimpering now, "don't kill me!"

"Tell us where the boy is."

"I don't know anything about a boy," the officer replied, twisting his head away and trying to get up. Melchiriel pinned his body down with one leg, pushing the stick harder into the man's neck. Gabi thought it looked like it might go through his skin at any moment.

"Don't lie to me," Melchiriel whispered menacingly, "Tell me the truth or I'll get my friend here to show you what a true Nephilim can really do…"

"Lord Damriel has him. He's keeping him alive until he can get his hands on her. That's all I know."

"Where?" Melchiriel's voice was barely audible

now.

"Somewhere at the school, but I've not been there. Please let me go."

Melchiriel put a little more pressure on the man's throat and Gabi watched as the officer's eyes rolled back in his head and he fell limply to the floor.

Melchiriel unclipped the radio from the man's stab vest and said: "Come on. We've only got a few minutes before he wakes up."

They walked over to the garage and Gabi lifted a plant pot next to the side door, revealing a key. She picked it up and unlocked the door. Rafa's car was still there, and the keys were hanging up next to the door.

Gabi clicked the central locking button and the car's indicators flashed together as the doors unlocked. "I can't drive yet," she said, handing the keys to Melchiriel who scooted around to the driver's door, opening it as Harriet climbed in the back.

"How are we going to get out of here without the other policeman seeing us?" Harriet asked.

"Leave that with me," Melchiriel replied holding up the police radio in his right hand, "Gabi, when I say, open the garage door, and be ready to jump in!"

Gabi went and stood by the garage door. She had been in here so many times. When she was much younger she used to be scared of the garage, with its spiders and cobwebs. But in recent years she and Rafa used to sit in the garage and talk, knowing it was somewhere their parents wouldn't hear them. She looked around, wondering if she'd ever be back here. In her head she said a silent goodbye.

Melchiriel's voice broke her trail of thought: "Ready?" he whispered. She nodded.

As Melchiriel pressed the talk button on the police radio it beeped three times in quick succession and Melchiriel, suddenly sounding quite urgent, said: "Quick! I'm in the garden in Woodcroft. They're here!"

He then turned the radio right down and waited.

In a matter of seconds Gabi heard a car door open

and slam shut.

She pictured the police officer scrambling to get out of the parked car in the street outside her house, slamming the door behind him, then running to the garden gate that was down the opposite side of the house.

"Now!" Melchiriel shouted, as he started the engine.

Gabi threw the garage door open in one easy movement and jumped in the front passenger seat. Melchiriel lifted his foot off the clutch and the little car roared out of the garage into the road. Melchiriel turned the steering wheel to the right and they drove away from everything Gabi had ever known. She turned and looked back in time to see a police car turn into the road, its lights flashing.

Something told her she would never see that house again.

CHAPTER SEVENTEEN

As Melchiriel turned out of Woodcroft Lane, Gabi closed her eyes and took a deep breath. Then, resolute, she turned to the angel and said: "I presume we're heading to school now? To find Rafa?"

"No," he replied, "you're not ready."

"But Rafa - "

"Rafa will be ok. You heard what the shadow said. Damriel's going to keep him alive until he gets his hands on you. And you're not ready for that yet."

"Then where are we going?"

"I don't know," he replied. He sounded weary. "I don't know."

There was silence for a few minutes as they traveled in the direction of the motorway.

Harriet broke the silence: "Should we go to my Nan's? I think we'd be safe there."

"What makes you say that?" Melchiriel asked.

"She lives by herself, in a cottage in the middle of nowhere. She hasn't got a mobile phone because she's always saying she's never needed one before, why would she need one now. She doesn't watch or read the news, because it's only ever bad news, and she's a really good cook. But I guess that last part isn't that important right now..." Her voice trailed off.

"Where does she live?"

"It's about an hour's drive from here. I'll put the address in for you."

She took her phone out of her bag and typed an address into Google maps then handed the phone to Gabi, who balanced it precariously on the dashboard behind the steering wheel in front of Melchiriel.

In the back, Harriet lay her head against the headrest and closed her eyes, feeling the gentle motion of the car as it made its way along the road. Gabi turned around to see her friend sleeping. Then she allowed herself to close her own eyes, just for a moment. Before she knew it, she was fast asleep.

Just under an hour later, the rumble of a cattle grid jolted them both awake. Melchiriel had turned the car into Harriet's grandmother's lane. The little private road was about a mile and a half long, and was clearly not maintained by anyone. The narrow road, lined by tall hedges either side would mean some careful reversing if they were to meet anyone coming the other way. The road itself was a mixture of dry dirt and big stones, churned up by the farmers that used this lane to get their tractors from field to field. There were deep grooves along the road, worn away over time by car tyres, creating a ridge down the centre of the road. Rafa's small car wasn't built for this type of road so Melchiriel had to drive off to one side, one set of wheels on the ridge, the other on the grass verge.

"We're nearly there," Harriet said, pushing herself up in her seat, and leaning forward, "her house is just up the hill and round the corner."

To their right the hedges broke, revealing a wide expanse of fields. The motorway and subsequent A-roads were nowhere to be seen as they drove slowly up the lane. They rounded a bend in the road, and Gabi saw a stone house at the top of the hill.

"There it is!" Harriet exclaimed.

Melchiriel drove up to the wooden gate and stopped. Harriet got out and almost ran to open it. As Melchiriel pulled into the small walled courtyard between the front of the house and a ramshackle barn opposite, Gabi watched as Harriet pressed the doorbell and an elderly lady came to the door.

The lady looked about seventy years old. She wasn't much taller than five foot tall and very slim. She had short, snow white hair and her wrinkled face burst into a smile when she laid eyes on her granddaughter.

The old lady's hands made a quick series of gestures and Harriet responded in a similar manner.

Harriet waved them over and they both got out of the car and walked towards the door.

"This is Nana O," she said, "She's deaf, but she's fairly good at lip-reading, so you don't need to use sign language with her. She can't speak though, so I'll translate. I've explained everything and she says we can stay as long as we need."

"Everything?" Melchiriel asked.

"Well…" Harriet paused, "I've explained that someone tried to kill Gabi by having her house burned down and that there are people trying to get her so we can't go to my parents' house as they'll think to look there. And I told her Melchiriel is a plain clothes police officer who is here to make sure Gabi's safe until they can find who did it…"

"So not quite *everything*…" Gabi said.

Nana O gestured for them to come into the house and they walked in to a large kitchen with a long table running down the middle of the room. A large Aga stove took up space against the wall on their right and in the middle of the table was a freshly baked loaf of bread, its delicious smell filling their senses. Gabi realised that breakfast felt like such a long time ago now.

Nana O gestured for them to sit down and set about cutting some slices of the crusty bloomer, then spread a thick layer of butter on each slice before handing them out.

As they tucked in to their lunch, Nana O signed to

Harriet. "She says it looks like we need to rest," she explained.

"She's not wrong," Melchiriel said, "your training starts tomorrow, Gabi."

"Training?" Gabi asked.

"Yep. You've got powers but you don't know how to use them yet. I can help."

"What about me?" Harriet said.

"We need you to start trying to find out as much as you can about where the sword of flames might be. Does your grandmother have internet?"

At this, Nana O signed angrily. Harriet laughed; "She says: 'I may be old and deaf, but I'm not stupid. Of course I have internet.'"

Melchiriel held his hands up: "Sorry Nana O, I was just asking!"

They finished their food and went through to the living room. Almost every bit of wall space was covered in books. From murder mysteries, to romance novels, to old leather-bound books with worn away titles, every shelf was full. There was nothing else in the room other than two armchairs, a sofa, and a coffee table that sat in the centre of the room between the seats on the polished wooden floor. A lampstand stood tall by one of the armchairs.

'I love reading.' Nana O signed.

"I can tell!" Gabi smiled, admiring all the books.

Nana O led them through the living room and up some stairs. She showed Melchiriel to his room then took the two girls through to a bedroom across the landing where there were two single beds.

"You take the one by the window," Harriet said, pointing to the bed furthest away from the door, "I always sleep in this one."

Gabi walked around the bed and sat on the edge, gazing out of the window for a moment before turning to Nana O. "Thank you," she said.

The elderly woman looked at her, smiled, and signed something.

"She says: 'My pleasure young woman. You've been through enough. You don't need to be so strong. Stop holding back. There's time to grieve. There's time to be sad. You don't have to hide your feelings."

With this something broke. Tears welled up in Gabi's eyes and ran down her face as she remembered breakfast with Uncle Mike and Auntie Em. She remembered Uncle Mike pushing her on the swing when she was six years old, and walking to the local pond to feed the ducks with Auntie Em. She remembered their laughter around the dining table every night. She remembered the deep conversations they would have about life, and faith, and philosophy, and science. And the stupid dad jokes Uncle Mike would tell whenever he could.

All gone forever.

Nana O sat on the bed beside her and put her arm around her shoulders. No words were needed. Gabi allowed herself to be held and felt the floodgates open. Resting her head on Nana O's shoulder her grief overtook her and there, safe in the gentle woman's embrace, she wept.

CHAPTER EIGHTEEN

"Leave him."

Damriel's voice echoed in the darkness where Rafa lay, shaking. Immediate relief flooded Rafa's body as he felt the shadows leave. What had felt like an eternity of pain, during which he had lost and regained consciousness countless times, ended as abruptly as it had begun.

He could not say how many times he had wished for death.

"Where is she?" Damriel said, his voice softer, "Tell me and all of this can end."

"I don't know," Rafa's voice was little more than a hoarse whisper, ravaged by his innumerable unheard screams, "I don't know."

"Have it your way. I take no pleasure in torturing you. Your sister... sorry, your cousin, is in grave danger. She is being led on a wild goose chase by an old acquaintance of mine. If his track record is anything to go by, he is undoubtedly going to get her killed."

"I don't know where she is," Rafa said, "I just want her to be safe."

The fallen angel removed a handkerchief from his inside breast pocket and crouched down. He gently wiped Rafa's bloodied, dirty face. "I'm not a monster.

I'm not the Devil. I just want to put an end to a curse that's been following me around for millennia. Your sister is the only one who can help me."

He stood up and took a step back; "I'll tell you what. I'll let you rest for tonight. No pain. No torture. I've even brought you some food."

Rafa felt the bonds around his wrists loosen and his hands were free. Damriel handed him a familiar brown bag with McDonald's golden arches clearly displayed. Inside, the Big Mac and fries were still warm. He took the cup of Coke gratefully and drank. He was thirstier than he had realised.

Damriel continued: "Rest tonight. There's no escape from this room. Think about how you might be able to help me find your sister, and in the morning, you can tell me. You know what will happen if you don't. Is that what you want?"

Rafa shook his head.

"Good. I'll see you in the morning."

With that there was silence and Rafa was alone.

Hungrily he shoved the Big Mac in his mouth, barely swallowing each mouthful before putting the next one in. When he finished his food, he untied his ankles and allowed himself just a few minutes of rest. There had to be a way out.

The room was almost completely dark. There was a small amount of light coming in through the narrow, painted window, but it was fading fast as the sun went down. Rafa stood, slowly. As he straightened his legs and arms, stiff from being tied up in the same position for hours, every muscle in his body seemed to be rebelling. Stumbling in the dark, he found his way to the wall and started systematically exploring the room.

The cold walls felt like they were made of brick. There were posters in places, although in this light there was no way he could read them. Feeling his way around the room he found the chairs he had briefly glimpsed earlier.

They were piled high in one corner of the room. He

dragged a pile of chairs and placed them under the window. Carefully climbing onto the pile of chairs, he was able to get his head level with the window. To his disappointment he discovered the window was not a traditional window with a pane of glass he could have broken, but rather three glass bricks. There was no way to open the window, or even break the glass.

Getting down again, he continued around the walls of the room, going around the shelving unit that was stood against the far wall, until he came to the door. The door was ancient and felt like it was made from very thick wood, held together with thick strips of metal. In place of a handle, there was only an iron ring. He pulled on the medieval door but it wouldn't budge. It was clearly locked or bolted from outside. He tried banging on the door, but each time his hand hit the door there was nothing but a dull thud. No one was going to hear him.

The sun had set and as darkness once again enveloped him, panic rose in his chest.

"HELP!" he shouted, "HELP!"

Nothing. No sound. No one came running. His cries echoed off the old walls, but travelled no further than the confines of the room. There really was no escape.

His foot brushed against something. Rafa crouched and felt around until his hand came to rest on something that brought him no comfort. His fingers felt the unmistakable shape of a leather shoe. It was still attached to a leg.

Forcing himself not to simply recoil in horror, Rafa searched the body discovering only the metal buttons that emblazoned every King Edward's School blazer.

Rafa withdrew, crawling in the darkness to the other side of the room where he curled up on the floor and closed his eyes.

After many hours, exhaustion overtook him and he fell into a fitful sleep.

CHAPTER NINETEEN

The smell of roast lamb and Yorkshire pudding woke Gabi from her sleep. She looked at her phone. It was seven PM. She was lying in her bed at Nana O's house. The sadness had been overwhelming and she had fallen asleep in Harriet's grandmother's arms. The rich aroma that wafted up the stairs was enough to make her forget her grief for a moment as she realised how hungry she was.

She went downstairs and saw Harriet and Melchiriel already sat at the table in the kitchen.

"Good to see you're joining us," Nana O signed, smiling as Harriet interpreted, "I've set you a place next to Harriet."

Gabi took her seat, "This looks incredible. Thank you." She placed her hand in front of her mouth and moved it away, the sign for "Thank you" and the only sign language she could remember.

Once Nana O had served their food they tucked in. Despite the late lunch, they were all hungrier than expected. They finished their first course and as Nana O was clearing their places to make room for dessert, Gabi said: "Melchiriel, you never finished telling me what happened to my mother…"

"You're right," the angel replied, "Where was I?"

"She had called you and you were going to meet at a café or something…"

"Little Chef. That's right."

Melchiriel sat back in his chair and continued; "So your mum called me and I agreed to meet her at Little Chef near Guildford. She sounded a bit panicky. She was bringing you and your dad in the car with her. Just as the conversation was coming to an end, I heard the sound of glass breaking and your mother shouted: 'They're here!' and the phone went dead. It was the last time I heard her voice.

I ran to my car and drove towards Little Chef. I knew the route she'd take so I decided to drive that route towards her house. The restaurant was a good nine or ten miles from where they had been living. I wanted to get to them as quickly as I could.

I came off the A3 onto one of the little 'B' roads, and drove down the country road towards their house.

As I turned a corner I saw their car come careening towards me, swerving all over the road. It was being followed by a police car with its blue lights and sirens going. Their car sped past me. Your dad was driving and I saw the panic in his eyes as he lost control. In my rearview mirror I saw the car skid right then flip over, rolling two or three times.

I slammed on the brakes and ran towards the car. It was upside down on its roof. I got there just as the police car pulled up behind it. You were in the back, strapped in to your car seat, crying. Your parents were both out cold. I tried to wake them but I couldn't. I opened the back door to get you out, and the police officer asked me what I was doing. I told him I was trying to save you and he looked irritated, but he took a few steps back and got on his radio while I got you out the back.

I heard him talking on the radio, saying he had just come across an accident. He didn't say anything about the fact he had been chasing the car down. I put you down on the opposite side of the road and went back to the car to check on your parents because the policeman wasn't doing anything but waiting. I saw the brake lines were cut. There was no way your dad could have stopped. As I got around to the driver's side, I saw a big puddle of fuel spilling out from the engine and flames lapping around the engine compartment.

There was nothing I could do. I ran over to protect you, reaching you just as the car exploded. More police cars arrived, along with an ambulance and firefighters. I saw that first police officer talking to a sergeant then return to his car. He walked past me as I held you. I don't know if he wanted me to hear him or whether he didn't realise I could, but I heard him say, quietly, but as clear as day: 'Hail Damriel'.

He got in his car and drove away.

There was a flurry of activity as I had to give a brief statement about what I'd seen and they took you away from me to hand over to your uncle and aunt.

I've been around as you've grown up, but haven't made myself obvious. It was important for you to have as normal a life as possible…"

Gabi looked confused; "But that's not how Uncle Mike and Auntie Em told me it happened…"

"They were told the police version… They didn't want anyone thinking they had caused a crash, especially one where two people had died, so they hid my statement, told Social Services they found you in your car seat outside the car, and that they had no idea how the accident happened. And they got away with it."

There was silence as the four of them sat around the table.

Nana O signed something angrily, making Harriet exclaim: "Nana!"

"What did she say?" Gabi asked.

Harriet half smiled as she told her: "Effing bastards."

There was a brief pause, then Gabi half smiled: "I couldn't have said it better myself."

Gabi felt relaxed. She felt safe, she wasn't hungry, and even though her parents' death was clearly no accident, somehow she felt an enormous sense of relief.

"Your training starts tomorrow," Melchiriel said, "so it'll be best to get an early night."

Gabi glanced down at her watch and realised it was almost nine o'clock in the evening, still early by any account, but, despite having slept all afternoon, she felt tired. Melchiriel helped Nana O clear the table and wash up, while Gabi and Harriet went to their room.

"It feels like we've been running for days," Harriet said, "it's hard to believe we only left school this morning…"

"I know," Gabi replied as she pulled the duvet up to her chin, "Hopefully tomorrow we can start trying to sort this whole mess out. And get Rafa back."

She rolled over, closed her eyes, and was soon fast asleep.

Nana O's Farm

CHAPTER TWENTY

The sun rose on the farmhouse, breaking through a crack in the curtains and shining brightly on Gabi's face. As she opened her eyes, for a few seconds she forgot where she was.

In that blissful moment, she somehow felt completely rested and at peace. She forgot about Rafa being missing, about the Sword of Flames, and about the fallen angel asleep in the room across the landing. She allowed herself to simply enjoy the feel of the warm sun on her skin before all those thoughts came rushing back in.

She rubbed her face and sat up. Harriet was still fast asleep, so she tiptoed around her bed and went downstairs. It was only six o'clock in the morning, but she had still slept for over nine hours. To her surprise, Nana O was already up, sat at the kitchen table drinking a cup of tea. She was just gazing out the window.

Gabi waved as she walked around the table and sat down opposite. Gabi couldn't sign so she pointed at her watch and shrugged as if to say: "Why are you up so early?"

Nana O picked up a pen that was lying on a newspaper in the middle of the table and chuckled to herself as she wrote on the corner of one of the pages: "I like the quiet." Gabi smiled at this and gave her a thumbs up. Nana O wasn't wrong. There was something peaceful about being sat in silence at the table in her kitchen.

A few minutes later Melchiriel walked in. "We've got to get some more clothes," he said, "I may look scruffy but I like my scruffiness to be clean…"

Gabi laughed; "Are we going to town then?"

"No," he replied, "we can't risk it. They'll be looking for us. They won't be looking for Harriet and her Nan. Plus, we've got to start your training."

He put some bread in the toaster, poured himself an instant coffee and sat down at the table; "And we've got to work out where this sword might be…"

Harriet walked in, rubbing her eyes; "Morning!" she yawned before signing "Hi, Nana," to her grandmother, "What's the plan today?"

"Gabi and I need to find somewhere I can teach her to use her abilities, and we need some clothes, and we need to work out where the sword of flames might be. Other than that, we've got no plans."

Gabi ignored his attempt at a joke. "H, if you go with Nana O to get us some clothes, that would be great. I don't know what 'training' I need," she said, "but I guess you're going to tell me, right?" She glanced at Melchiriel, who nodded before she continued, "And I don't know where to start with finding the sword, but if you could find out what happened in my great-great-grandfather's book, that might at least tell us where Rafa might be hidden in the school…"

Melchiriel smiled. "The wisdom of Solomon himself," he said, "Sounds like a good plan. Eat up. We need to get started."

Gabi ate a couple of slices of toast with marmalade, which had always been her favourite ever since she was a little girl. Auntie Em used to make homemade marmalade and the slightly bitter sweet orange jam reminded her of breakfast back in Capel Cross. She washed it down with a glass of apple juice and stood up; "Right, let's go."

Melchiriel followed her out of the kitchen into the field behind the house. There were no other houses for as far as the eye could see. In the distance she could see a large hill, known by the locals as One Tree Hill. Silhouetted against the blue sky was the single oak tree that grew on its summit, high above the surrounding farmers' fields.

"What's first?" she asked.

"Slow down," Melchiriel replied, "you're not going to master your abilities in a day. We need to work out what you can do, and what you still need to learn."

"Remind me what abilities the Nephilim have again. Strength and speed wasn't it?"

"Among others. But it depends on each person. Some people have incredible strength and only a little of the others. Others are incredibly wise, but lack speed. Or incredibly fast, but not as strong. You get the picture."

"Well, let's find out what I've got so we can get on with finding Rafa," Gabi said. A real sense of urgency had completely replaced any peace or calm she had felt when she woke up.

"Alright!" Melchiriel said, "Let's start with strength. Follow me."

He walked her to the edge of the field where a large tree had fallen over in recent winds. The trunk was about three and a half feet wide and the roots were taller than both of them. The angel pointed at the tree: "Shall we start small?"

"There's no way I can move that!"

"You won't know unless you try…"

Gabi crouched down near the end furthest from the roots and placed both hands under the trunk. She could feel the rough bark on her palms. She closed her eyes and straightened her legs.

Or at least, she tried to straighten her legs. The tree didn't budge. Not even one millimeter.

"Like I said; there's no way I can move that."

"That's because you don't believe you can move it," Melchiriel said, "You need to have faith. It's been said that with faith the size of a mustard seed you can move mountains. This is just a tree."

Standing beside her, he put his hand on her shoulder and continued; "You've used this strength before. There's no reason you can't use it again."

"When?"

"How did you escape the police station?"

"Yeah, but he just lost his balance…"

"What about the guard on the train?"

"I don't know…"

"Every time you were in danger you tapped into your hidden strength. You just need to learn how to do it on command. Try again."

Gabi reached down, gripping the underside of the tree trunk and tried again. It still didn't budge.

"Keep trying."

Hours dragged by as attempt after attempt failed. The tree wouldn't budge.

Shortly before midday, Melchiriel said: "I'm tired. Maybe I was wrong. Maybe you're not Nephilim. Or you just don't want to save your cousin enough. I don't know. I'm going in." He turned back towards the house and started walking.

From behind him there was an almighty crack as the tree trunk broke away from its roots and flew over Melchiriel's head, landing a few metres ahead of him. He smiled and turned around.

"Nicely done. Now put it back."

Lifting the tree a second time was far easier, and within minutes Gabi was picking up the tree as though it were nothing more than a twig.

She placed it back on the edge of the woods, grinning: "What's next?"

"It's almost lunch time, but I guess there's a little time to work on your speed…"

"Is that how I got from the police station back to school in such little time?"

"Maybe. Let's find out," he smiled, "I should probably hold your phone though, in case it falls out of your pocket while you're running."

Gabi took her iPhone out of her pocket and handed it to him; "Look after it."

"Of course," he replied, "now, catch!"

Gabi watched in horror as her iPhone flew high into the air. He had clearly thrown it as far away as he could, right across the field towards the stone wall that ran around the far edge.

The phone landed gently in her outstretched hands and she looked up to see Melchiriel standing exactly where he had been. She, however, was now almost a hundred metres away, by the stone wall.

"What the hell are you doing?" she shouted.

"Just giving you some motivation!" he laughed.

"You douche. It's not funny," she replied, although she couldn't help smiling, just a little.

"Hold on to that feeling," Melchiriel said, as he jogged over to where she was standing, "you need to be able to harness that without me throwing your phone."

"How does it work?" Gabi asked, "I don't even remember moving my legs to run."

"It's referred to as angelic transportation," he said, "it's mentioned in different legends, and in the Bible. It's why angels can suddenly appear and why people can be carried off to different places. There's a story of a man called Philip who baptized a eunuch in a lake in the desert. As soon as he had done this, he was 'snatched' away and appeared in a town called Azotus. Many people think he was teleported, like you see in those Star Trek shows, but the truth is, an angel was sent to take him away so that the eunuch would not tempt him with rewards for his work."

"OK…"

"Here's how it works: Your body can take you, very quickly, to where you need to go, but it must be somewhere you have seen with your eyes. You can't go through walls, or any other sort of nonsense, but you can get across water, due to the speed you travel, just as long as you can visualise where you need to be."

"OK. Sounds simple enough. Where shall I go?"

Melchiriel scanned the horizon and stopped at One Tree Hill. "See that tree?" he said, "Ready? Steady. Go!"

He allowed himself to blink but by the time he opened his eyes Gabi was gone and he could see a tiny figure waving back at him from the top of the hill. He waved and the figure vanished, as Gabi reappeared next to him, a fraction of a second later.

"You know what I said about not mastering this stuff in a day?" he said, "I guess I was wrong!"

Gabi grinned. "Can we go get Rafa now?"

"We need to find the sword first, but soon. Very soon. Let's have some lunch first, and find out how the others are getting on."

Melchiriel blinked and Gabi was gone.

Three minutes later he walked into the kitchen to find Gabi putting some spreads on the table she had just set.

"I could get used to this speed thing," she said, smiling.

With this the door from the living room burst open and Harriet ran into the room, slamming the Alchemist's Journal down on the table.

"You'll never believe what I've found!"

CHAPTER TWENTY-ONE

"So," Harriet said, "first things first, I didn't go to town with Nana, I stayed here. She said it would be safer, which made sense to me, so I started reading your however many greats grandad's book. Melc, how much do you know about Ravi dos Santos?"

Melchiriel smiled; "Not as much as I'd like. I saw him once, boarding a ship on one of his many trips, but never caught up with him. I do know he was well respected, both as a teacher and as a person, although some people thought he may have lost his mind a little towards the end…"

"I keep forgetting you're really old!" Harriet said, laughing, "Anyway, so, we found his book hidden in the school library. They were going to throw it out. We had only just started reading it when Gabi got the text message that made her run home.

We had just got to a bit where Ravi had arrived in Brazil where he was looking for something that was hidden in a cave somewhere. We didn't know what he was looking for because he had written it in a weird code. Or so I thought. This morning I went through it and used an app that lets me translate things by taking a picture of it. I thought I'd do that and Gabi, you'll never believe what he was looking for - only the Sword of Flames!" Harriet could barely contain her excitement:

"The gemstone he talked about at the start," she pointed to the text that read 'אוֹר', "that's actually Hebrew, not some weird code, like we thought, and it means 'LIGHT'. Then later on he talks about The Army of Shadows." She pointed at the text that said 'צבא הצללים'.

"And here's what got me properly excited," she carried on, pointing at the text a little before that read 'חרב אש', "he was literally looking for what Google translated as 'Fire Sword'. That's too much of a coincidence. It's got to be the Sword of Flames!"

Melchiriel leaned over her shoulder to get a better look at the book. "That's incredible," he said, "that's definitely hebrew and yes, it could be translated fire sword or sword of flames. And it was in Brazil?"

"It was," Harriet replied, "but it's been moved. I'll catch you up. Grab a seat."

The three of them sat down around the kitchen table and Harriet started reading:

14ᵗʰ August 1786

The last few days have been very eventful. I am writing this from the safety of my ship, but allow me to start at the beginning.

Following an early start the morning after I arrived, my guide took me out into the jungle. It was very hot and I was plagued by mosquitos and other flying insects. We walked for three hours, deep into the trees along narrow footpaths that Guilherme told me had been made by the local indigenous people. Our horse was laden with rations and digging equipment.

We eventually reached a rope bridge across a river. The cave was just over the other side. We tied the horse up as there was no way she would be able to cross over, took our rucksacks, and started our crossing.

The bridge itself appeared not to have been used for years. The wooden slats were rotten in places and the rope was frayed. To say I was apprehensive was an understatement. I have been in many situations in my advanced years, but I am still not keen on the idea of placing myself in a situation where I could plummet to my death.

Far below us I could see crocodiles in the river. Guilherme was ahead of me and almost lost his footing when one of the wooden slats gave way beneath him, the wood tumbling lazily into the water below. However, we reached the other side of the river, unscathed and continued the journey.

As we continued down the path we lost sight of the bridge. After a few minutes, we heard our horse whinny one last time, and then silence. We were all alone in the jungle.

After about an hour or so, Guilherme suddenly ducked under a tree branch and headed into the undergrowth on his left. I followed, and within moments came across a fairly non-descript cave. The entrance to the cave was barely big enough for a man to fit through. I entered the cave and followed a path deep into the side of the mountain.

It wasn't long before the light from the entrance faded and we had to light our torches to find our way. It felt like an eternity but we eventually reached the end of the tunnel which opened out into a large chamber. High above us was a small opening through which it appeared a single ray of sunlight was able to shine, illuminating a pool of water that reflected the light in rippling patterns across the walls of the cave.

I leaned over the water and there it was, deep in the water - a sword. I could see the handle and hilt were gilded with beautiful gems. On the wall behind the pool I saw the following words, carved in Portuguese into the rock:

A espada dos anjos se esconde aqui
Submerso seguro para alguém de coração puro
Quando as sombras entrarem, a chama ela produz
Pois a escuridão não existe onde se encontra uma luz

The English translates as follows:

Here you find the sword of angels
Safely submerged for one with a pure heart

When the shadows enter it produces a flame
For darkness doesn't exist wherever light is found.

I feel it is more poetic in its original language, but the sentiment is clear. I knew I had found what I'd been searching for.

I plunged my hand into the pool but the sword was beyond my reach. Removing my outer clothing I left Guilherme by the water and climbed in to the pool. I dove beneath the clear crystalline water and found the sword was far deeper than it appeared. I couldn't reach it on my first attempt so returned to the surface and refilled my lungs.

I dove again and was able to wrap my fingers around the hilt before struggling back towards the surface, my lungs burning.

As I climbed out of the pool, Guilherme was quiet. He was simply staring at me, his eyes vacant and dark. Before I realised something was wrong, he attacked me making me drop the sword. He was acting like a rabid dog, possessed by something. He quickly overpowered me and I found myself on my back on the floor as the previously gentle priest wrapped his hands around my neck.

I felt darkness creeping in and reached out until my fingers found the sword and with my final ounce of strength I plunged the sword into his side. He went limp and released me as guilt and fear took hold of me.

I know it was the only thing I could have done, but I fear this feeling of guilt will never leave me.

I ran from the cave, leaving Guilherme there. I couldn't carry him and there was no saving him, but I knew I had to get out of there. I wrapped the sword and strapped it to my back under my rucksack before heading back out into the jungle.

The path back to the crossing felt interminably long. Without Guilherme to guide me I had the constant feeling I had taken the wrong turning. I felt uneasy the whole way, but I kept the river on my left so I knew eventually I'd find my way back to the bridge.

I had been walking for about an hour and had become accustomed to the noises of the jungle. There were animals, birds, and insects constantly creating a cacophony of noise that my brain had somehow filtered into the background, but then I heard the unmistakable sound of a twig snapping.

I stopped to listen and held my breath. There was no one behind me on the path and I couldn't see anyone ahead or in the bushes around me.

As I took a step forward something whistled past my ear, striking the tree just in front of me. It was a dart, decorated with colourful feathers, embedded deeply in the bark. Without a moment's thought I started to run and it felt like the jungle erupted behind me. There was a flurry of noise as a tribe of indigenous people seemed to emerge from the bushes behind me.

More darts whistled past, followed by an arrow. I could hear them hollering, letting out angry war cries as they chased down the path behind me. I rounded a corner, taking the opportunity to look back over my shoulder. There were about seven or eight half naked men chasing me. They had straight black hair, cut in a straight line across their foreheads, and their tanned faces were painted in black and red paint. Suddenly the bridge was in sight, only a hundred yards or so ahead.

I ran as fast as my ancient legs would take me and started crossing the rope bridge. I was about half way across when I felt a rock strike me in the back, knocking me to my knees. I grabbed hold of the ropes and pulled myself up, turning to see my pursuers stepping on to the bridge.

I hurried to the other side, they were only a matter of metres behind me now. I stepped off onto solid ground and turned, pulling the sword from its coverings. As I swung the sword down through the first rope one of the natives shouted out. His voice was thick and gravelly and his words were unmistakably English: "Watch out! I'm coming! For you, for your children, and your children's children!"

I sliced through the second rope and the bridge fell away. In that moment I looked my attacker in the eyes and something changed. In the second before he plummeted into the river with his fellow tribesmen I could have sworn I saw the hatred in his eyes fade, replaced with a look of confused panic.

And then he fell, swept away by the rushing river below. I can only hope and pray he survived.

This is when I noticed our horse. She was lying on her side, her head pulled back at an unnatural angle, her neck broken.

I don't know what kind of animal can break a horse's neck like that, but I wasn't going to wait to find out so I ran. I ran for what felt like forever, but I eventually broke free of the jungle out into the open from where I could see the lights of the city in the distance.

Tiredness overcame me so I found a gap behind some rocks along the edge of the road. I had planned to sleep until the morning, out of sight, and safe from any larger animals, but I'd barely been asleep for more than a few minutes when I heard voices.

There were three men, all speaking Portuguese, and they were clearly drunk.

I tried to make myself as small as possible so they wouldn't see me. I was hoping they would just walk past, but now I am certain this sword draws evil like a moth to a flame.

As the footsteps drew nearer I hunkered down in my makeshift shelter, trying to fade into the shadows when I noticed a faint glow. It was coming from directly in front of me. The אוֹר jewel in my pendant appeared to be glowing. As the men drew nearer it became brighter and brighter. I tried to hide it by clasping my hand around it, which helped, but the glow shone through my skin so my hand was bright red. The light was so bright it was almost as if I could see right through my hand.

One of the men found me and let out a mighty shout. I jumped to my feet, instinctively clutching the swords hilt as the other men surrounded me. My pendant was glowing so bright now I could see every line on their faces, every wrinkle, every blemish. I could smell the alcohol on their breath and see the light reflecting off the steel of their swords. Yet their eyes were pools of darkness, devoid of any life or movement.

They were all around me. I had no choice but to fight.

As the one who found me raised his sword to strike I raised my sword and was instantly bathed in a light brighter than I had ever seen before. As the white light radiated from the sword, illuminating everything around me I was almost blinded. The men screamed in pain as if the light was red hot, and they fell to the floor, dropping their swords.

Keeping the sword raised I picked up my bag and stepped out from behind the rocks. One of the men started convulsing and screaming. He suddenly turned his head towards me, his eyes wide open, and hollow. This is when I saw what I had previously only heard rumours about - a shadow. It flowed from the man's eyes and took the form of a man before me, but it could come no closer. I took a step towards it and it recoiled.

I took flight, and as I turned to run I heard the same voice I had heard at the bridge: "Your children! And your children's children…"

As soon as I was a short distance away the light faded and I found myself once again in darkness.

I found my way back to Guilherme's church where I hid, unhindered for two days, until I could buy myself passage on this ship, The Three Brothers. I have hidden the sword in the depths of my trunk where I am hopeful it will attract no more attention.

I have feigned an illness so I do not need to leave the cabin and the kind captain of this ship has brought me my dinner. Upon my return I must find somewhere to hide this sword where the darkness will not find it.

5th January 1787

It has been several months since my return from Brazil. My health has taken a turn for the worst. I am finally starting to feel my age. I hope I have been successful in my mission. חרב אש has been hidden in the most sacred place in the heart of England's primary capital cathedral. It is my desire that it remain there until someone with the strength to vanquish darkness can wield it. I pray it is not discovered by the shadows lest they destroy it or learn to harness its power.

I have entrusted my pendant to my grand-daughter, Grace, who embodies everything that is beautiful in the world. She reflects in her life, the beauty of her name, carries my precious wife's smile, and my daughter's love, and a fortitude that is all her own.

I am grateful to be convalescing in my quarters at the

school I love where I have been able to teach a few lessons this academic year, but sadly my strength is failing me now.

Harriet closed the book. "This is where his entries finish. According to that website we saw, he died in 1787 in a fire, and someone found his book in a safe in his classroom. I guess he was able to get to his classroom one last time."

Gabi was quiet for a moment as she allowed the words of her great-great-great-grandfather to sink in. "At least we know where the sword was hidden," she said quietly, turning to Melchiriel, "When can we leave for London?"

CHAPTER TWENTY-TWO

"London?" Melchiriel asked, "Why London?"

"Weren't you listening? That's where he said the sword's hidden," Gabi grabbed the book from Harriet's hands and scanned the page, "Here, look, it's *'been hidden in the most sacred place in England's primary capital cathedral.'*" She turned the book around, pointing at the text on the page.

"St Paul's!" Harriet exclaimed, "Of course! The main capital cathedral."

"That's all good," Melchiriel said, "but where in the cathedral is it hidden? How are we going to get in to London without drawing attention to ourselves? And what are you going to do once you have the sword. You've barely started to scratch the surface of your powers. We need you to be as strong as you can be."

"I get that," Gabi replied, "but I can't just sit here for days while Rafa is being kept prisoner somewhere. Who knows what they're doing to him? Are they feeding him? Torturing him? I can't just sit here."

Nana O signed something.

"She says we wouldn't get to London in time today anyway," Harriet translated, "and we should stay, at least until tomorrow morning, before heading up there."

Melchiriel frowned; "I think tomorrow's too soon. Gabi needs more training."

"You saw what I can do today," Gabi said, standing up and walking to the door, "I'm going tomorrow morning, whether you come with me or not."

"Fine, fine," Melchiriel said, "I clearly can't stop you. But you must spend the rest of the afternoon training. Deal?"

"Fine."

Harriet stood up and started clearing some the plates from the table. "We need to know where Rafa's hidden though. Even if we turn up at school with the sword, I don't think we'll be able to just wander around checking every classroom until we find him…"

"You're right. And he won't be hidden in a classroom anyway. The school's been around for hundreds of years. There's probably hidden tunnels and passages all over the place. I take it you don't know any?" Melchiriel replied.

"There were always rumours of a door into the tower, but I've never actually gone looking for it," Gabi said.

"Shag Tower" Harriet laughed, "the rumours were always about who the latest sixth formers were to have gone up there to have sex… I've never met anyone who has actually been up there though."

"Wait," Gabi said, "Mr Cox said something about a map that was stolen from his office. He said there were secret tunnels on it and that Ravi had drawn the map himself."

Melchiriel nodded; "We need that map. I can only assume it's been stolen by one of the Shadows. Is there a copy anywhere?"

Gabi shook her head: "I don't think so. Mr Cox seemed very upset. Said it was a one off."

Nana O stood up suddenly and went over to her kitchen drawer. She pulled out a pile of leaflets and started going through them. Eventually she found what she was looking for and handed it to Harriet.

"The British Museum?" Harriet said, opening the leaflet up.

Nana O pointed at a list of exhibitions and Harriet read: "Special exhibition: Architecture Through the Ages - Architectural Blueprints from 1500 to Modern Day. When's this leaflet from?"

Nana O signed.

"1986?!?" Harriet exclaimed, "This exhibit will be long gone! It was only there for three weeks."

Melchiriel reached over and took the leaflet. "They never throw anything away. And even if they don't have it anymore, they'll know where to find it," he said.

"We don't even know if they had the school's blueprints in the exhibit," Gabi added.

"No," Melchiriel continued, "But if anyone knows where there might be a copy, they will."

"Great!" Harriet said, reaching for her phone, "I'll call them and find out."

"No!" Melchiriel reached across, snatching the phone from her hand, "Sorry. We don't know who they'll talk to. If Damriel's soldiers find out where we're going, they'll be there waiting. It's best we turn up unannounced."

Harriet shot Gabi a glance: "So-rry," she said, sarcasm dripping from her tongue, "just trying to help."

"We just can't take the risk. I didn't mean to over react," he apologised.

"OK," Gabi interjected, "just to make sure I've got the plan straight. Tomorrow morning we're heading to London to the British Museum where we'll get the map then head to St Paul's to find the sword, then save Rafa?"

Melchiriel nodded: "You make it sound simpler than I expect it will be, but yes. That's the plan."

"Great. Let's go do that training." With that she grabbed a bread roll from the kitchen side and walked out the door into the garden, Melchiriel following after.

In the darkness, Rafa sat alone. Damriel had been

true to his word. He had brought him food and had allowed him to rest that night. Damriel had called it rest, but really Rafa had had little more than a few hours' sleep. Having discovered the body, fear had taken over and nightmares came every time his eyelids closed.

And now, Damriel stood before him, tall and strong while Rafa had no strength left in him.

"Where is she?" Damriel demanded, "Where would she go?"

"I still don't know," Rafa whispered, a smile curling at the edges of his lips, "Have you tried the library? Her and Harriet are always in the libra-" He stopped, realising his mistake.

"Harriet?" Damriel asked, a smile spreading across his entire face, "That'll do nicely."

He turned to his right and whispered something under his breath and all light was blotted out for a moment as shadows left the room at his bidding.

Damriel then motioned with his hand, as if calling someone closer, and darkness, once again, closed in. Rafa felt the shadows invading every pore of his being and for the second time in two days he experienced pain that made him long for death, knowing it wouldn't come.

Gabi spent the afternoon in the field with Melchiriel, practising her newly discovered skills. She quickly found her strength could be activated at will and lifting heavier and heavier objects became a fun challenge.

She began with the tree trunk they had first worked on in the morning, which was heavy enough but easy to lift.

"What about that then? Could you lift that?" Melchiriel was pointing at a tractor in the neighbouring farmer's field.

"I guess…" she replied "won't the farmer mind?"

"Not if he doesn't see us…" Melchiriel smiled at her and winked. She noticed how blue his eyes were. How they wrinkled a little at the edges when he smiled. In that fleeting moment she felt like she had known him her whole life.

"Come on," he said, ducking under the fence out into the little lane separated the farmer's field from where they were standing. Gabi laughed as she stooped under the wire he was holding out of her way and they crossed the road together.

The tractor proved no challenge at all. It was even easier than the tree trunk.

"What about that?" Gabi said, pointing to a combine harvester parked at the far end of the field, "I'll race you!"

In the blink of an eye she found herself next to the giant green machine. It was about four or five times bigger than the tractor, with enormous blades on the front that it used for harvesting wheat. It must have weighed about fifteen tons.

Gabi examined the machine, looking for the perfect place to grip. Deciding to grab two handles on the rear of the machine, she planted her feet to steady herself. Gabi closed her eyes, waiting for the surge of power to come. It started with the faintest of crackling in the base of her skull then a sudden rush, like lightning coursing down through her chest, and arms, and legs. And she lifted.

The gargantuan emerald machinery towered high above her head, casting a shadow far across the field. Melchiriel jogged up next to her. "Very impressive. Very impressive indeed!" he laughed, "Now maybe put it down slowly…"

Gabi lowered the combine harvester onto the ground, elated. In that moment, for some reason, all her troubles and worries faded into the background and she felt like a great weight had lifted. "Thank you," she said, turning to Melchiriel, "Thank you." She threw her arms around him as he awkwardly took a step back, arms out by his side. Gripping him tightly she buried her head in his chest and felt his hand gently patting her on the back. She remembered Uncle Mike's gentle arms around her. The way he had comforted her whenever she hurt herself as a little girl, and again later on when she was rejected by that boy in secondary school. His arms had always been there for her when she needed them. Melchiriel wasn't as good at hugging as Uncle Mike, but right now this was exactly what she needed.

"Oi! You two!" a gruff voice pulled her back into the present and she looked over Melc's shoulder to see a rather large man with a big ginger beard walking up the field towards them. "What are you doing on my land?" he shouted, loading a cartridge into his shotgun that lay broken open over his left forearm.

Gabi grabbed Melchiriel's hand, "I think we need to get out of here." Before Melchiriel could even open his mouth to agree, they were back in Nana O's field.

Across the lane, in the distance, a very confused farmer stood alone next to his combine harvester, scratching his head. Years later he would still tell the story of the two thieves who vanished right in front of his eyes.

No one ever believed him.

CHAPTER TWENTY-THREE

The sun rose over the misty fields of the small holding, its golden rays once again breaking through the gap in the curtain, waking Gabi from a deep sleep. She smiled. She hadn't slept that deeply since before the fire. Apprehension and excitement filled her body as she threw back the covers and quickly got dressed.

She chose something inconspicuous, a black t-shirt and blue jeans, after all today they were going to London, hopefully to put an end to this whole horrid situation. She didn't want to wear anything that might draw any attention.

She gathered up her clothes from the floor by her bed, remembering how Auntie Em would always complain about her "floordrobe". She stuffed them in a holdall, picked up her phone from the bedside table, and went downstairs.

The other three were already up. Melchiriel, dressed in his usual attire, scruffy dirty jeans, an old band t-shirt (The Ramones today) and his long coat, was sat at the table. Harriet, in a plain white summer dress with a thin leather belt, was pouring juice into the four glasses on the table as the sunshine caught the daffodils in the vase next to the toast rack. There were six slices of toast stood up neatly in the rack in the middle of the table next to the butter and the homemade marmalade.

Nana O, who was standing by the hob cooking the scrambled egg, turned and waved as Gabi came in.

"Morning!" Gabi said, pulling out a chair opposite Melchiriel, "What's the plan today then?"

"We need to get the plans for the school and find the Sword," he replied, "I'd suggest getting the plans first. We don't want to be walking around London all day with a massive sword. If anything will draw attention to us, it'll be that."

"Won't we have to carry the sword at some point anyway?" Harriet asked.

"Yes, but if we can make that as short a time as possible, we'll hopefully be able to get in and out without being spotted by the police or by any of Damriel's demons."

"That makes sense," Gabi said, "What time does the museum open?"

"Ten a.m," Melchiriel said, pulling a tube map from his pocket, "My suggestion is that we park at Clapham Junction and get a train into the city itself. There's free parking there, and if our number plate's been compromised at all, there are fewer cameras to see us that far out. We can use public transport to get to the museum."

As he said this the early morning sun went behind a cloud, blocking out some of the light in the kitchen.

"It's due to rain this afternoon," he went on, "so let's eat up and get going. We should be able to get to Clapham by about eight-thirty if we leave soon. That'll give us plenty of time to get to the museum and be there for when it opens."

Nana O brought the scrambled egg over and served Harriet first. "Eat up, girls," Nana O's voice was tired and raspy as she served Gabi her eggs. Gabi picked up her fork to start on her breakfast when she noticed Harriet staring at her grandmother.

Nana O was standing dead straight and completely still, right next to Melchiriel, her angry, darkened eyes fixed on Gabi opposite. Her rasping voice continued: "You're not going anywhere."

Her arm swung at an incredible speed, slamming the pan into the side of Melchiriel's head, sending him flying off his chair onto the floor where he lay motionless.

Gabi and Harriet leapt to their feet, pushing their chairs back. "What are you doing?" Harriet shouted, her face flushed red, tears beginning to form, "Nana O, what the hell?"

"Your Nana's gone," Nana O said, moving her jaw from side to side, as if it hadn't been used in a long time, "Her body's mine now."

The two young women watched as Harriet's grandmother reached towards the knife block and pulled out a carving knife then lumbered towards them around the table.

"I've got this!" Gabi said, "Go see if Melc's alright."

"Just don't hurt her," Harriet pleaded, "She's still my Nan."

Gabi picked up one of the kitchen chairs and threw it at the old lady. It struck hard and broke into several splintered pieces, bouncing off Nana O's arm doing nothing to stop her from advancing. Gabi picked up the chair Harriet had been sat on and ran at her friend's grandmother, pushing her up against the wall, knocking into the welsh dresser, sending display plates flying, smashing on the ground around them.

Nana O's right hand was still gripping the handle of the carving knife and she lashed out. Gabi pulled away but the knife went straight into her shoulder, slicing through her skin, deep into the muscle. She cried out in pain, dropping the chair and stumbling back. The possessed woman's eyes flashed red with anger and she threw the chair aside. She lurched towards Gabi, her movements stilted. Her left hand grabbed Gabi's throat and her fingers squeezed with a supernatural strength, closing her airways. Gabi fell to her knees as Nana O raised the knife above her head.

Gabi's vision started fading as darkness crept in, clouding her sight, when, from seemingly out of nowhere, Harriet appeared behind her grandmother.

The vase that usually stood in the middle of the kitchen table was held high in her right hand. "Get off her!" she cried as the vase came smashing down on Nana O's head.

The knife fell from the old woman's hand as her body jerked forwards and she released her grip on Gabi's throat, slumping to the ground.

"I'm sorry Nana," Harriet whispered as she put her right forearm around her grandmother's throat, "I'm really sorry." She locked her right wrist in the crook of her left elbow and squeezed until her grandmother's body stopped moving. She was out cold.

"Quick," Gabi said, pushing herself to her feet, "Put her in the pantry, she won't be knocked out for long."

Harriet lifted the unconscious woman by her armpits, while Gabi grabbed her feet and together they carried her into the large pantry at the far end of the kitchen. As they placed her on the floor she started to come to, her eyes flickering open. Harriet paused for a moment, looking down at her grandmother. "Come on!" Gabi said, standing in the door way, "We have to leave her!"

With that the old woman sprung to her feet, all signs of age and frailty gone. Gabi reached into the pantry and grabbed Harriet's belt. She pulled her out of the pantry, and slammed the door shut behind her. She slid the old bolts shut as the old woman let out a blood curdling scream and started hammering on the door: "Let me out! Let me out! We're coming for you. We're coming for you!"

"We need to go." Gabi felt strangely calm as she backed away from the door, taking hold of Harriet's hand and leading her shell-shocked friend to where Melchiriel was lying on the floor.

He groaned slightly as they approached him and he opened his eyes, muttering "What happened?"

"We'll fill you in in the car," Gabi replied, picking up her bag from by the door and slinging it over her good shoulder, "can you drive?"

"I think so."

The two girls helped him to his feet and they staggered out of the house.

As the front door closed behind them they could still hear the banging from the pantry and, as they drove away, the old woman's unearthly screams echoed across the fields.

Gabi fixed her eyes on the road ahead, her whispered words barely audible: "It'll be ok… It'll be ok."

CHAPTER TWENTY-FOUR

The journey to London was silent. No one dared speak for fear that even a single word might open the floodgates, allowing sadness to take over, extinguishing any flicker of hope they may have been harbouring.

After what felt like an age, Melc pulled off the motorway and the view from their windows was filled once again with the familiar sight of residential streets. Semi-detached houses at first then, as they drove further into the giant city, terraced houses and high-rise buildings became more prevalent.

"I'll park at Clapham Junction" Melchiriel said, breaking the silence, "it's outside the congestion charge area so we're less likely to be recognised by the number plate cameras…"

He brought the car to a stop in a narrow street next to a fenced off council estate. It wasn't the sort of place you'd feel safe walking through alone at night but that morning there was nothing out of the ordinary. People were simply getting on with what they did every day, oblivious to everything the three inhabitants of the little car had been through. Children were waving goodbye to their parents, a mother, smoking a cigarette in her pyjamas and dressing gown, was carrying a bottle of milk and a loaf of bread in one hand, while balancing a toddler on her hip with the other hand, clearly making her way home from the local shop. Business men and women were standing quietly in line at the bus stop next to factory workers in overalls, school children, and track suited youths, all waiting for the bus - and all completely ignorant to the danger their world was in.

Leaving the car in the parking bay, the trio joined the crowds of people walking up the steps to Clapham Junction, the busiest train station in the whole of British Rail's train network.

"Three adult Day Travel Cards, please" Melc said to the sour faced woman behind the Perspex window in the ticket office. He pulled a wad of cash from his pocket and handed it over as she rolled her eyes, then printed the tickets. "Next time use a card," she said, without any hint of a smile.

"I'm pretty certain she's a demon…" he said with a wry smile as he handed the girls a ticket each, "Let's go."

They followed him through the ticket barriers and onto Platform 3. A train was due in the next three minutes.

Gabi couldn't help but feel like all eyes were on them as they waited for the train to pull in. A man with a briefcase standing a few feet away checked his watch then glanced at her, catching her eye. A teenage girl wearing tracksuit trousers and a vest top, looked over in her direction and stopped chewing her gum for just a moment. A woman in a power suit and trainers stared at the three of them for longer than what would be considered polite, her high heeled shoes sticking out the top of her handbag.

"I think we're being watched," Gabi said, "I don't like it…"

"We've been careful," Melc replied, "It may just be nerves, but I'll keep an eye out. Let's stay close, but maybe try to look like we're not together…"

The train came to a stop and the doors opened with a hiss. It was only a couple of minutes late. Boarding the train, they stood close, but not next to each other.

It was rush hour so it was standing room only in the carriage. The train lurched forward and they were on their way into central London.

As the train clattered along the tracks, Gabi felt more and more uncomfortable. The carriage continuously shifted from left to right, making her stumble, other passengers knocking into her, jostling her. She reached out to grab hold of the hand rail to steady herself. As she did another hand folded over hers, clamping it in place.

Before she could call the others for help her eyes locked onto the piercing brown eyes of an old man. "Don't be afraid," he said "don't call for help."

Something in the way he spoke to her made it impossible for her to cry out.

He continued: "Things aren't as they seem. You won't find what you're looking for here… Only trouble. But remember: you're stronger than you know…"

The train passed under a bridge and cast the train into shadow for a fraction of a second, and with that, the old man was gone.

Gabi looked to her left and saw Melc standing there, tall and strong, his back to the doors as his eyes slowly moved up and down the carriage, scanning for trouble. Harriet on the other hand was sat opposite, head down, her arms resting on her knees. Gabi thought she had never seen her looking sadder.

There was a commotion from further down the carriage and Gabi swung her head to the right to see what was happening. "Don't touch me!" The woman in the power suit and trainers looked angry. A heavy-set man directly in front of her looked taken aback; "I didn't do anything…" The woman pushed him square in the chest and he stumbled back as she turned and made her way through the crowded train in Gabi's direction. She stopped directly in front of Gabi, her back turned. "Men…" Gabi heard her mutter under her breath.

Gabi felt herself relax a little. Maybe the woman wasn't out to get them after all.

She turned her head to check on Melchiriel and Harriet.

But they weren't there.

They were gone.

CHAPTER TWENTY-FIVE

Gabi felt panic rising, her heart pounding in her ears as blood rushed to her head. She wanted to scream, to cry, to curl up in a ball on the floor of that moving train. Where were they? How could she have lost them?

Something inside stopped her from doing any of the things her instincts were telling her. Instead she mustered all her courage and, taking a deep breath, slowly and calmly made her way to where she had last seen Melchiriel by the train doors.

None of the other passengers appeared perturbed, as though nothing had happened. It was almost as if two of their fellow travellers hadn't simply vanished from a moving train, in the centre of London, right in front of their eyes.

There was no sign of any disturbance; no signs of a scuffle or fight. Where Harriet had been sat, there was now a middle-aged man in his fifties reading that morning's copy of the Times.

As the train pulled in to its final destination at London Waterloo, Gabi wondered if maybe they hadn't just moved a little further down the train to spread their group out a little.

The doors opened with that familiar hiss and Gabi alighted the train, carefully stepping over the gap between the train and the platform. Standing back a little from the train, she waited, watching as passengers streamed out of every door in every carriage. She watched the passengers as they continued on their daily commute, desperately hoping for a glimpse of Melchiriel's long dark coat, or Harriet's red hair.

As the last passengers stepped off the train it was clear they were definitely gone. There was no one left on the platform other than Gabi and the woman in the power suit and trainers, who was deep in conversation on her phone. Gabi could hear snippets of what she was saying: "Yes, we're still on track to meet our targets… of course… I won't lose sight of the objective… I know how important this is…"

Their eyes met for a moment and the woman flashed a quick smile at Gabi before turning away, returning to her call. Gabi started walking towards the exit, reaching into her pocket for her ticket.

She didn't know what to do. She could hand herself in to the police and try to explain what was happening, but they wouldn't believe her. Worst of all, if any of them did believe her, they would most likely be possessed by one of Damriel's demons, and she'd be trapped.

Turning left out of the main entrance to Waterloo, Gabi started walking along Cab Road, towards the City. Within moments she realised there were footsteps behind her, following her. She quickened her pace, until she was almost at a pedestrian crossing, across the road from the familiar sight of a KFC restaurant built into an old bridge.

As she prepared to cross the road she risked a glance over her shoulder just in time to see a fist flying towards her face. The woman in the power suit wasn't holding back. The first punch knocked Gabi back, the second made her knees buckle as she fell to the floor.

The woman wasted no time. Reaching down she grabbed Gabi's torso, swung her around and flung her backwards, sending her flying into the entrance to an abandoned car park under a derelict office block.

Gabi's back struck the corrugated metal of the shutter doors before her right shoulder hit the floor, followed immediately by her right temple. Blood started flowing from a cut on her head, and the woman's right trainer struck her in the face. Gabi's head snapped back as her nose broke.

The woman pulled her foot back then swung it towards her face again. Without a second thought Gabi's instincts kicked in. She rolled towards the kick, blocking it while wrapping her arms around the woman's two legs. Gabi pushed her bodyweight forward, trapping the woman's feet with her arms. The weight of her body forced the woman to lose her balance, stumble and fall backwards.

The woman's head bounced off the kerb with a thud and Gabi straddled her, leaning forward and placing her right forearm across the possessed woman's neck. She could see the darkness in her eyes - the woman was one of *them*.

Gabi shifted forward a little, allowing herself to place a little extra weight on her throat, until she heard a gurgling, rasping sound as the woman struggled for breath.

"Where are they?" Gabi shouted, "Where have they gone?"

The woman tried to speak but couldn't get the words out.

Gabi released the pressure on the demon's throat, just enough to hear: "You'll never find them…"

"Where are they?" Gabi asked again, anger rising up from deep within her, "You know what happens if I kill your host…" She increased pressure on the demon's throat and the woman's eyes started rolling backwards.

"OK…" it rasped, "OK… He has them. He's going to kill them, and your brother. He wanted me to bring you to him so you could watch…"

"At the school?"

With that the woman's body convulsed violently

and a shadow slipped out, silently gliding across the road into the darkness of the abandoned car park. The woman's body then lay still, her breathing shallow.

Gabi scrambled to her feet, head still bleeding. She ran across the pedestrian crossing and under the bridge, pausing only to tell a traffic warden to call an ambulance for the woman.

She didn't wait to see if he actually did.

Meanwhile, elsewhere, Harriet could feel strong arms around her, restraining her, stopping her from moving. No amount of kicking or straining made any difference to her captors. She remained restrained and immobile.

An impenetrable darkness surrounded her and her screams vanished into an abyss of silence the moment any sound passed her lips.

A deep despair set in as the darkness thickened and after a while she stopped struggling as, resigned to her fate, the fight left her.

CHAPTER TWENTY-SIX

When Gabi eventually stopped running she found herself standing outside a McDonald's restaurant. A man in a suit carrying a cup of coffee emblazoned with the golden arches logo paused as he walked past her. "Are you ok?" he asked, sounding concerned, "Do you need some help? Or an ambulance?"

"I'm ok…" she replied, turning away, "I'm fine."

"Ok…" he said, shrugging as he walked off. Gabi caught a glimpse of her face, reflected in the window of the restaurant. It was a mess. She had blood all around her mouth and nose, her eyes were bruised and puffy and her hair was matted and chaotic. No wonder the man had stopped to ask how she was.

Head down, Gabi walked into McDonald's, avoiding eye contact with any of the hungry customers. They were all too preoccupied inputting their orders on the giant menu screens to notice the teenaged girl making her way to the toilets. Gabi opened the door to the disabled toilet and went in. This way she could avoid being seen by anyone else.

She leant close to the mirror over the sink to assess the damage. Her nose was clearly broken, the blood around her mouth had dried now, but was still very obvious, and she had two black eyes. Her shoulder was still throbbing where Nana O had stabbed her.

Her only hope of finding her friends was to follow the original plan, but there was no way she'd be able to get into the British Museum looking like this.

The cold water running from the tap seemed to bring her a sense of calm and she paused for a moment, watching as the water filled her cupped hand and overflowed into the sink. She brought her cupped hands up, splashing water on her injured face.

As she wiped the blood away she felt a strange tingling under her skin – the lightest of pins and needles. She watched in amazement as the bruises started to fade. Wherever she washed seemed to heal at the touch of the water.

She filled her cupped hands with more water and brought them up to her nose. Instantly her nose returned to its usual place, no longer broken. She did the same with her eyes and the relief was immediate. Her bruises faded at the touch of her hands and within moments her face was completely healed, as was her shoulder.

She allowed herself to stare at her freshly healed face in amazement before flattening down her dishevelled hair. Then she composed herself, and left the bathroom stall.

Stepping out into the busy London street Gabi realised she had no idea how to get to the British Museum. She had no money for a taxi and no idea what bus or underground to catch with the underground ticket she still had in her jeans pocket.

But this was London. There would undoubtedly be some sort of tourist office, or information stand nearby. She turned right and there, in front of her, was London Bridge Station. She had run far further than she'd thought.

She walked through the doors and found a station guard standing by the barriers.

"Excuse me," she said, "what's best way to get to the British Museum?"

The guard, who didn't take his eyes off the people queuing to get through the barriers, said: "The quickest way is to get yourself to the High Street, catch a bus to Liverpool Street Station, then get the Central Line to Holborn. It's about five minutes' walk from there…"

"Thanks," Gabi said, turning to walk away.

The guard looked up. "Wait a minute…" he said, "are you ok?"

Gabi turned back: "I'm fine."

"You've got blood on your clothes. You're a mess. They'll never let you in looking like that…"

"I'm O.K.," she said.

"Wait there," the guard said, grabbing her arm as he reached for his radio.

Gabi didn't wait.

She ran.

In a blink of an eye she was standing in London Bridge Borough High Street.

The training Melchiriel had given her over the past couple of days came flooding back and suddenly she had a plan.

She walked along the high street until she found a Tesco's supermarket. This would be the easiest way of getting by unnoticed. She kept her head down as she walked into the shop and went straight to the clothing section. She quickly selected a pair of jeans in her size, and another black hooded top.

There was no one standing at the entrance to the fitting rooms, so Gabi walked in unseen and changed out of her bloodied clothes into the fresh new ones.

She remembered having been to the British museum once before. She had been about six or seven years old and her uncle and aunt had taken her and Rafa into London for the day. She'd been desperate to go to Madame Tussaud's and the London Dungeon, but Uncle Mike and Auntie Em had been adamant they should "Get some culture!" and had insisted they all go to the British Museum instead.

She remembered standing outside the black metal

railings looking up at the giant pillars that lined the front of the building, making the museum look like an ancient Greek temple. Again, she closed her eyes and there she was: standing outside the gates of the British museum.

Staff at Tesco's would later find a pile of blood-stained clothes in one of the fitting rooms and no evidence anywhere of anyone having left.

Gabi looked up at the imposing building and walked up the large steps towards the entrance.

She pushed the glass door open and walked in.

CHAPTER TWENTY-SEVEN

Gabi was in the giant entrance hall of the museum. The floor and walls were all white marble, and the ceiling was simply a giant glass dome that allowed the room to be flooded with sunlight. There were several groups of people milling around, deciding where to go. To her left she saw a group of school children in uniform with an increasingly frustrated teacher shouting: "Put your coats in the cloakroom, then find your group… And stay together!"

To her right a group of four women in their late fifties or early sixties were talking about heading to the Stonehenge exhibition, and how the coffee shop at Stonehenge sold delicious cakes. There were a few other groups that looked like university students. No one paid any attention to her, she was just another hoodie-wearing teenager.

Gabi scanned the room until she saw what she was looking for. She wasn't interested in the "Samsung Discovery Centre" or the "Stonehenge Exhibition", both directly in front of her, but rather she was looking for the desk she saw to her far right. Above it was a single word: "Information".

She walked straight up to the desk where she was greeted by a woman in her late thirties wearing a British

Museum uniform - a dark blue t-shirt with a light blue logo. Her name tag read *Joanne*. "Hi, welcome to the British Museum, how can I help?" Joanne said.

Suddenly feeling nervous, Gabi said: "Thanks... I'm just wondering if you can help... I'm doing a school project for history and I need to find out what I can about my school..."

"OK..." the woman replied, "and why are you at the British Museum for that? Surely you can find out what you need at the local library? We really only tend to have exhibits from around the world, so I don't know if I'll be able to help..."

"I've tried my local library," she lied "but there's nothing there that's any help, just stuff I already knew..."

"Right..."

"And my nan said you used to have an exhibit here about architecture through the ages. I was just wondering if you still have that."

"If we do, it was definitely before my time," the woman said, smiling as her face lit up, "but it's so good to see someone your age taking such an interest in local history. Give me a minute and I'll see what I can find out."

She picked up a phone and Gabi heard her say: "Is Gerald in today? Great. Can he come to the info desk, I'm wondering if he might be able to help me with a customer..."

She turned back to Gabi and said: "Gerald's one of our curators. He's been here for a long time. If anyone can help, it'll be him."

A few minutes later an old man wearing a tweed jacket and a faded red bow tie shuffled over to the desk. He was quite short for a man, only a little taller than Gabi herself. He had a mop of bright white hair, bright blue eyes, and a friendly smile. Gabi instantly warmed to him.

"Hello young lady," he said stretching out his slightly shaky hand towards her.

Gabi shook his hand and smiled: "Hello, I'm Gabi."

"Gerald," he replied, "It's a pleasure to meet you. I understand you've got some questions about your school's architecture?"

"Yes please… I'm trying to find out how much my school has changed since it was built to now, but I can't find the original design anywhere, and my nan said you had an exhibit about British architecture, so I was hoping you might be able to help…"

The old man put his hand on his chin and tapped his cheek with his index finger: "Hmmm… I do remember that exhibition. It was a long time ago, maybe 1985 or 1986. I'm sure we've still got the exhibits somewhere in our files. We don't tend to throw anything away… Follow me!"

He turned and walked across the entrance hall towards a little door marked "STAFF ONLY". Gabi followed and watched as he typed a code into a keypad then opened the door.

He held the door for her and she walked through.

Gerald waved his arms in a grand gesture and winked as he said: "Welcome to the secret underbelly of the British Museum! Also known as 'The Staff Area' where we take our breaks and eat our lunch!"

He chuckled and said: "It's also where we keep our archives. It's a bit of a walk though…"

He led her through the staff room, past a coffee table littered with unwashed mugs, to a door that opened onto a long corridor. Gabi followed him down the corridor that lit up as they walked along it. She noticed the lights turned off behind them so only the section of corridor they were in was lit up at any one point. "They're motion sensors to save energy," Gerald said, "they can be a bit annoying. I personally quite like to be able to see where I'm going!"

They had walked through the corridors for about three or four minutes when Gerald came to an abrupt stop and said: "Here we are."

He took a bunch of keys from his pocket. Fumbling

through the keys, he muttered "I can never remember which one it is…" After trying three different keys, he finally unlocked a door on their left and swung it open, leaving the bunch of keys dangling in the lock. "That way I don't need to find it again when we leave," he muttered to himself.

Gabi followed him into a room lined with filing cabinets. There was a large table in the centre of the room. She suddenly realised she was all alone with a strange man, in a private part of a very large building, and the only person who knew she was there was an information desk worker who probably wouldn't even notice if she never came back.

"What's your school called?" Gerald asked.

"King Edward's School," she replied, "It's in Capel Cross in Surrey."

Gerald moved over to a filing cabinet at the far end of the room and put on a pair of white cotton gloves. The filing cabinet was a much wider than standard filing cabinets. He opened the middle drawer. His fingers moved quickly over the different files, flicking them towards him as he tried to find what he was looking for. "King Edward's, King Edward's…" he muttered as he looked, "Ah, here it is!" he finally exclaimed, pulling out a large architect's drawing. The paper had yellowed with age, and Gabi could see the ink had faded with time. Gerald brought the plans over to the large table and placed the architect's drawing flat on the table.

"Obviously, it'd be easier to find differences if you had brought a modern day plan, but is there anything obvious to you?" Gerald asked.

Gabi stared at the plans, focusing on the older parts of the school. There was nothing obvious around the science block, nothing of note around the swimming pool, although she did find it interesting that the swimming pool had always been in the same location.

Then she spotted it. Under Queen Anne House there appeared to be the faint outline of a room that stood out from the building above. There was also a clear corridor running from there all the way to the main building at the front of school. The tunnel came to a stop directly below the centre of the building, just to the side of the entrance archway. She could also see steps hidden inside the archway walls. She'd never seen those before.

They led directly to the tunnel.

CHAPTER TWENTY-EIGHT

Harriet could hear noises in the darkness; quiet groaning that sounded more animal than human.

"Melchiriel?" she whispered, "Are you there?"

From the darkness she heard another groan. "Melc, is that you?"

"It's me…" came the whispered reply.

Trying to stand, Harriet found her ankles were bound, so she reached out into the darkness, pulling herself on her hands and knees towards where Melchiriel's voice had come from.

She could feel the weight of the chain that bound her as it dragged behind her, allowing her to move only about four feet from the wall. As she slowly moved across the room, she heard Melchiriel grunt as he tried to shuffle towards her. They had been chained to adjacent walls and after a few moments of blind scrambling Harriet found Melchiriel's arm. He clearly wasn't wearing his coat anymore as she could feel the skin of his arm. It was wet and his arm hairs were matted and sticky.

"What happened?" she asked.

"I fought back…" he said, his voice strained as he struggled to continue, "As we went under a bridge I saw something grab you and you went limp. It dragged you down the carriage and through the door towards the next carriage. I chased after you but they surrounded me, pulling me through the darkness into the air. I tried to fight, but I felt their claws ripping in to me, tearing my clothes and my skin. They were just too strong. Next thing I know I'm waking up here…"

Harriet felt his body slump back to the floor.

They sat in silence for a moment.

"Where are we?" Harriet asked, breaking the silence.

"I don't know…"

"You're back at King Edward's."

Harriet instantly recognised the voice.

"Rafa?" she said, unable to disguise the excitement in her voice.

"Yeah. It's me. They've kept me here for days… Where's Gabi?"

"I don't know," Harriet said, "We were on a train heading into London when they grabbed us and brought us here."

Rafa listened in silence as, over the next hour or so, Harriet told him everything. She told him about the fire, the Army of Shadows, the Sword of Flames, and the Nephilim.

"No wonder they want to find her," Rafa said when she finished, "Their leader is determined to get to Gabi. He wouldn't tell me why she was so important, but as hard as all of this is to believe, if it's true, then it's clear why he wants her."

"We need to find a way to get out of here," Melchiriel rasped.

"I've tried," Rafa said, "There's no way out. Everything's locked and now we're chained to the walls…"

"There's always a way," Melchiriel replied.

Deep under the British Museum, Gabi turned to Gerald and said: "Any chance I could get a copy of these plans?"

"I'm not allowed to do that, Gabi, really sorry," he

replied, "but you can take a photo if you have a camera or a phone?"

"I lost my phone on the way here…" Gabi lied, "Can you find me a piece of paper and a pencil and I'll just copy the part that's important…"

"Of course." Gerald turned and walked to a desk in the far corner of the room.

Seizing the opportunity, Gabi grabbed the architect's plans from the table and sprinted towards the door. "I'm so sorry!" she shouted as she pulled the door closed behind her, locking it with the key the old man had left hanging in the key hole.

She hurried down the corridor, back the way she'd come, folding the ancient paper up as she did, only slowing as she approached the staff room. She tucked the folded plans down the back of her waistband, hiding it under her top as she composed herself before walking back out into the public area of the museum.

As calmly as she could she headed back towards the main entrance.

"Was Gerald able to help you?" Joanne's voice rang clear across the large room from the information desk.

Gabi turned towards her. "Yes, thank you," she said, then paused "He asked me to ask you to go and check on him in about 15 minutes. He said he was feeling a bit tired and was going to take a break in the staff room after he cleared up in the archives room…"

"Good old Gerald! He is getting on a bit!" Joanne smiled, shaking her head.

Gabi forced herself to smile back, "Thanks again."

She walked out through the large doors into the bright London sunshine. She was careful to stop herself from breaking into a run as she descended the steps and headed back out, past the security guards at the gates, onto the busy city streets.

There was a Starbucks directly opposite the entrance to the museum but there was no way she felt safe enough to stop there to study the plans properly, so she turned left, then right, into a road called Bury Place.

About halfway down Bury Place, on the left, she saw an old bookshop with a little coffee shop in the back corner. Aware there would be people looking for her before too long, Gabi ducked into the shop. Making sure she could see the door, Gabi went further into the shop, pretending to be looking for a book. The shop extended much farther than it had looked from the outside, long rows of bookshelves with every type of book imaginable. Prince Harry's autobiography sat side by side with an old John Grisham novel, nestled among a number of older leather-bound classics; Pride and Prejudice, Little Women, and even a second edition copy of The Jungle Book. There didn't seem to be any "system" at all for how these books were organised.

Slowly moving along the shelves, keeping one eye on the books and one on the door, it wasn't long before she heard shouting from the street outside. Two burly men wearing fluorescent tabards ran past the shop, their radios crackling. "She can't be too far!" she heard one of them say.

She stepped back, even further into shop, when an old man's voice startled her.

"How can I help you?"

The shop owner was an older gentleman, his bright white hair neatly combed into a side parting. He was wearing a shirt that was slightly too large for his small frame. A navy-blue bow tie, tied neatly around his neck, perfectly matched his well-worn waistcoat and navy blue trousers. His piercing brown eyes drew her gaze to him and made her feel like she might have known him for an eternity.

"How can I help?" he repeated. His faint foreign accent implied he had lived in the UK for a very long time, and she couldn't quite place where he might be from. He smiled and the corner of his eyes crinkled, revealing laughter lines reserved only for the faces of the fortunate few who have lived a life well lived. There was a warmth in his voice that set her at ease and she stammered: "I just need somewhere safe to wait for a few minutes…"

"Make yourself at home," he said, "would you like a cup of tea?"

"I haven't got any money…"

"Don't you worry about that," he smiled, "this one's on me. Grab a seat. Rest a while." He gestured towards the empty coffee shop area at the back of the shop and, feeling grateful, Gabi pulled up a chair and sat down. She took the folded paper from her waist band and placed it on the table to stop it getting more creased than it had to be, then took a deep breath, resting her head in her hands.

Closing her eyes, she allowed herself to stop for just a moment.

"Here you go," the shop owner said, putting a teacup on a saucer down in front of her. He filled her cup from a delicate white teapot, then put the teapot down in the centre of the table. "You look troubled," he said.

"I've not had the easiest of days…" she replied.

"Want to talk about it? I've been told I'm quite a good listener, although I'm not sure my wife always agrees!"

There was something about him that put Gabi at ease. She wasn't sure if it was how gently he spoke, the way he moved so slowly and deliberately, or just his slightly wonky bow tie, but she felt she could trust him.

"My name's Yuri," he said, sitting at the chair opposite, "What shall I call you?"

"Gabi," she replied, "my name's Gabi."

"What's been going on?" he asked.

Before she even realised what she was doing, Gabi started telling him everything. Yuri sat quietly as she told him about the fire, about the strange man who had followed her, about the police chasing her. She told him about Harriet's grandmother, about how she had attacked them. She told him about how they had been attacked on the train and how she'd had to fight the businesswoman on the road outside Waterloo Station.

She was careful to leave out some of the more fantastical elements of the story, after all, who would actually believe her?

She had been talking for about an hour, during which time Yuri had refilled her cup at least twice, when he finally interrupted her. "Who's after you?" he asked, "and more importantly, what do they want from you?"

Gabi hesitated.

"You wouldn't believe me if I told you," she said.

Yuri reached across the table, gently taking hold of her hands. He looked her straight in the eyes: "I've lived through more than you can imagine," he said, "try me."

So she did. She told him everything Melchiriel had told her. She told him about the Army of Shadows, about the Sword of Flames, about Damriel, and finally she told him about how Melchiriel believed she was the last descendant of the Nephilim.

Yuri's kind eyes had not flinched at any point during her story. He simply listened with a quiet intensity she had never experienced before.

When she finished speaking it was late afternoon. Yuri stood quietly and said: "You've been through so much. Let me help you find what you're looking for."

He walked to the far corner of the bookshop. Gabi watched as he reached, on tiptoes, and pulled down a dusty volume from the top shelf of a bookcase tucked away in the corner.

The leather-bound book's cover was worn and tatty and she could see its pages were yellowed and crispy, the way old paper goes when it's been left in the sun for years. Yuri handed her the book. "This might help you."

"Chronicles of the Nephilim," Gabi said, reading the large gothic print on the cover, "Where did you get this?"

"I've had it on my shelves for a very long time,' he replied, "I suppose it was just waiting for the right person to need it…"

"Thank you," she said, carefully opening the book to

its title page, "I should probably get going though, I've taken up enough of your time."

"Don't be silly. You needed to talk. Let me check the coast is clear."

As he said this, Gabi heard the sound of sirens as three police cars screeched to a stop outside.

From her chair at the back of the shop she watched through the large display window as six police officers in bright yellow coats and body armour got out of their cars and started walking towards the door.

CHAPTER TWENTY-NINE

Gabi felt panic rising in her chest as the police officers walked slowly towards the entrance of the book shop. Wondering, for a moment, if maybe Yuri had called them, she noticed a tall, slim man wearing a long black coat standing next to a police officer on the other side of the road. He was pointing at the shop.

"Someone must have seen me come in here," she whispered, crouching with Yuri behind her chair, "I'm so sorry."

"Don't be," Yuri replied in a hushed tone, "They can't come in unless I let them in, and I'll have you out of here before that happens…"

"They don't need a warrant to come into a shop, Yuri, I've seen enough police shows to know that much!"

"Trust me," he said, a twinkle in his eyes, "you'll see."

From their hiding spot at the back of the shop, Gabi watched as the first police officer reached the door. He put his gloved hand on the handle and pushed. The door didn't budge.

He tried again, pushing harder this time. Still the door wouldn't open. He took a step back and barged the door hard with his right shoulder. Still nothing.

Raising a clenched fist, the police officer banged on the door five times, making the frame rattle. "Open up!" he shouted, "It's the police!"

They didn't move.

"It's the police!" the officer shouted again, "We know you're in there! You were seen coming in!"

Gabi saw him gesturing to his colleagues who had gone back to the car and were now returning, one of them carrying a large red metal door ram.

"Follow me," Yuri said, "but stay low."

Crouching down, Gabi followed him behind the counter at the back of the shop. She took one last look at the door. The police officer with the ram was surveying the door.

"Don't worry," Yuri whispered, "It won't work!"

Behind the counter, Yuri reached up and pressed a button directly under the till. Gabi heard a soft click and turned to see the lower half of a bookshelf behind her had moved out ever so slightly. Yuri swung the bookshelf open revealing the entrance to a long corridor.

"Head that way," he said pointing into the corridor, "at the end of the corridor you'll find a door that will lead you out onto the street. Wait in the corridor for ten minutes and I'll come meet you."

Gabi crawled through the opening into the tunnel and the shelves swung shut behind her.

In the distance she heard the muffled sound of Yuri's voice saying; "Calm down, calm down, I'm coming. Can't an old man go to the toilet in peace?"

She crawled for a few feet before the corridor opened up, giving her plenty of space to stand. The passageway was about fifty metres long, the same as four or five double-decker buses placed end to end. Its walls were lined with dark wood panelling, the type of panelling you find in old civic buildings and theatres. Old fashioned light fittings lit her way, set at regular intervals along one side of the corridor. The corridor itself wasn't much wider than a large doorway. It would have been a struggle for two people to walk past each other, and the dark wood panelled walls added to her feelings of claustrophobia.

She rushed to the end of the long corridor where she found the door Yuri had mentioned. The door had no handle and no clear way of opening it. "It must open from the other side…" she muttered to herself.

Checking her watch, she saw it was almost five-thirty in the afternoon. *Ten minutes,* he had said. She sat down with her back to the wall and waited.

5:40 came and went.

As did 5:50.

At 6 PM Gabi stood and crept back to the corridor's entrance where she had come in. She couldn't hear anything from the other side of the secret doorway so she pushed it hard. It didn't budge. There were no obvious handles or buttons to push and after a few minutes frantically running her hands around the edges of the door, her eyes struggling to hold back tears, Gabi took a deep breath. There was no point panicking. It wouldn't make things any better.

Returning to the far end of the corridor where Yuri had said he'd meet her, Gabi sat back down.

Her fingers reached for her mother's necklace and wrapped around the pendant hanging at her neck. The familiar feel of the pendant brought her unexpected comfort.

In the half-light of the corridor's old bulbs Gabi's eyes became heavy and her tiredness caught up with her. She allowed her eyes to close as sleep drifted in.

Suddenly the door burst open with a bang, pulling Gabi from her sleep. "Come on! Come on!" Yuri said, his voice urgent, "We've got to go!" Rubbing her eyes Gabi glanced at her watch. It was 8:13 PM. She had been asleep for two hours.

Yuri's bow tie was hanging, untied, around his unbuttoned collar. His shirt was ripped and his waistcoat was missing. His right trouser leg was torn at the knee. There was blood around his nose and his knuckles were grazed.

"What happened?" Gabi said, struggling to get to her feet, her stiff back and legs putting up painful resistance.

"No time to explain, I'll tell you when we're safe."

He took hold of her hand, his grip surprisingly strong for someone so old, and helped her stand. He put his head out the door, looked left and right, then said: "Let's go."

With that he set off running at speed along an alleyway, still holding Gabi's hand firmly in his, ensuring she kept up with him. The alleyway ran between tall buildings, lined with large industrial bins and rubbish bags. Graffiti covered the poorly maintained walls of the buildings they ran past, broken up only by old metal doors, rusty and dirty. Unfolded cardboard boxes betrayed the secret sleeping places of the city's homeless.

They crossed road after road, carefully avoiding moving cars and other pedestrians. Keeping off the main roads as much as possible, Yuri took her down alleyways and side streets rather than main thoroughfares until Gabi was well and truly lost in the darkening city.

Finally, they ducked under a narrow archway that led to a well-maintained courtyard. A rack of chained up bicycles were lit by a single lamppost in the middle of the cobbled street. Georgian blocks of flats lined every side of the courtyard, their entrances flanked by faded white pillars and adorned with building names: 'Charity Court', 'Charity House', and an unnamed building on her left.

"In here," Yuri said, stopping by a non-descript door on the left. There was no one in the courtyard as Yuri looked around then crouched down. He lifted the corner of one of the paving stones next to the door and when he stood up he had a key in his hand. "Good, it's still there!"

He unlocked the door and ushered Gabi through,

following her in and shutting the door behind them. He locked the door and slid three bolts across. He rested his back against the door and sighed deeply, his shoulders dropping, his hands on his knees. "Home," he said, "We're home. Welcome."

Yuri reached to the wall on his right and flicked a switch turning the lights on.

Gabi saw she was standing in a fairly narrow entrance hallway. The stairs on the left side took up half the width of the room and were carpeted with the same dark red patterned carpet as the rest of the room. The carpet reminded her of carpets she had seen in old fashioned pubs. The walls were covered in wall paper that looked like it had come from the sixties or seventies. The lower half of the walls were a dark red while the upper half was made up of vertical cream and light red stripes. There was a large painting in a wooden frame hanging on the wall to the right of the front door. The artist had clearly been working with contrasts, depicting a dark wooded area, with twisted gnarled trees on the left side and a beautiful, lush green garden on the right-hand side, separated by a cave from which the rays of a bright light were escaping into the darkness.

The room was filled with the delicious smell of freshly baked bread.

The sound of a door opening at the end of the hall startled her as an elderly woman, who must have been in her late seventies, opened the kitchen door and said: "Yuri, is that you? I've been worried…"

"Yes, dear, it's me. I'm back," he replied. "Gabi, this is my wife, Naomi. Na, this is Gabi, she needs a place to stay."

Naomi can't have been more than five foot tall. She was wearing a simple white ankle length skirt and a flowery blouse. She reminded Gabi of the warm welcoming grandmother figures she had seen described in every story book or Disney movie she had read or seen growing up. Naomi dried her hands with the tea towel she was carrying, hung it on the door handle and flung her arms wide as she rushed across the room: "Of course my dear," she said, wrapping her arms around Gabi, who could only stand there stunned, "you look absolutely famished. Let's get you some food. Come, come!"

She took hold of Gabi's hand and pulled her towards the kitchen. She shot a look at Yuri as she walked past, "And you can tell me what happened to you!" she said.

The kitchen was simple and homely. Pine cupboard doors set apart by the dark granite or slate worktops and pale blue walls. There was a large white fridge on the left by the door as they went in. Gabi could see a freshly baked loaf of bread sat on a chopping board on the kitchen side, its top perfectly dusted with flour, steam gently rising above it.

"Grab a seat you two," Naomi said, indicating a table at the other end of the room, "I'll bring stuff over."

Gabi took a seat on one side of the dark wooden table. The table was only big enough to fit two chairs down each side and was clearly used regularly, its once polished top now scuffed and marked with age. A white vase filled with tulips took pride of place in the centre of the table.

Behind the table, along the wall, were several shelves filled with ancient books.

Yuri took a seat at the head of the table to Gabi's right.

Gabi suddenly realised how hungry she was as Naomi put down a freshly brewed pot of tea and three mugs. She returned moments later with a tray carrying three plates, three butter knives, a large jar of strawberry jam, a block of butter, and a pile of the thickest slices of fresh bread Gabi had ever seen.

Naomi placed them down in the middle of the table. "Tuck in!" she said, "It's 'stretch or starve' in our house!"

Gabi helped herself to a plate and marveled as the butter melted into the warm slice of bread she'd placed on it. She added a thick layer of the dark red jam and took a big bite. It was delicious. She leaned back in her chair, feeling a sense of peace she hadn't experienced in what felt like days.

There was quiet for a few minutes as the three of them sat together enjoying the warm bread until Naomi broke the silence: "Now, Yuri, are you going to tell me what on Earth is going on? What happened to you? And who are we hiding Gabi from?"

"I hate to say this, Na, but it looks like they're back…"

The exit from the passage

CHAPTER THIRTY

Yuri took a deep breath and started: "Gabi came into the shop earlier today. I could tell she was in trouble…"

Gabi didn't speak while Yuri told Naomi everything. From the fire at her house, to the Army of Shadows, to her being the last Nephilim, and her search for the Sword of Flames, Yuri missed nothing out.

Naomi was quiet for a moment, and appeared to be considering everything she had just been told, then said: "You did the right thing bringing her here. Of course you did. She needs to be safe." She turned to Gabi and added: "And we'll do everything we can to help you."

"Thank you," Gabi replied, "I am wondering what happened to you though, Yuri."

"Oh, it's not that bad," he said, dismissing her question with a wave of his hand.

"She's right to ask," Naomi added, "plus, I want to know too. So, tell us."

"OK. As you know, I got Gabi to safety in the tunnel. I forgot to tell her how to open the door at the other end, which, as it turns out, was a good thing, but I'll get to that. Anyway, she was in the tunnel and I went to let the police in."

"When did you lock the door?" Gabi asked, "I don't

remember you locking the door when I was in there."

"That's a little complicated to explain," Yuri said, "but suffice to say, no one comes into my shop if I don't want them in there. Anyhow, I opened the door for the officers and four of them came in and stood around me. They did the usual, asking my name, taking down details. Don't worry, I didn't tell them where I lived, just that they could normally reach me at the shop if they needed to.

They told me a violent criminal had assaulted and falsely imprisoned an old man at the British Museum and that she had been seen to come into the shop."

"I never assaulted him!" Gabi said, then added "I may have locked him in a room though…"

"I know, I know, don't worry," Yuri said, "I told them a young girl had come in earlier and explained you had looked through some books and then left. Of course, they didn't believe me. One of them was very condescending and spoke to me like I was stupid, saying something like 'You won't mind if we look round then?' I told him it was fine and to make himself at home, but to be careful because some of the books were old. He really wound me up when he said 'They're just old books, but yeah, we'll be careful…'. They started pulling bookshelves out, moving them away from each other, as if you could somehow hide between back to back bookshelves… I just stood back and let them search. I knew they wouldn't find you. I thought they had finished when one of the officers shouted 'Sarge, look I think I found something!' He was standing by the table we had been sat at and was holding the map of your school…"

"Oh no!" Gabi said, a feeling of dread filled her whole body. It had all been for nothing. "I'm such an idiot. There isn't another copy anywhere."

"Don't worry," Yuri said, reaching behind him, "You don't need another copy." He placed a police evidence bag on the table in front of her. Through the clear plastic bag she could see the folded paper she had left behind.

"How?" Gabi asked.

"I'm getting there. Patience..."

Yuri poured himself another mug of tea and continued: "When they found the map and brought it over to the sergeant, the young officer pointed out the stamp on the top left that said 'PROPERTY OF THE BRITISH MUSEUM' and the sergeant told him to arrest me. So he did. I got arrested for theft and for handling stolen property, or something like that, and they put handcuffs on me. Thankfully he put them on the front. I presume he didn't think I was much of a threat. I waited while he put the map in the evidence bag, then he walked me to the car. He searched me, even looking under my bow tie, put me in the back seat, and put the seat belt across me. Then he put the evidence bag on the seat in the back next to me and sat in the front. In fairness, he was quite pleasant with me, he was very polite and tried to reassure me. He said we'd get this matter sorted quickly and that they wouldn't keep me at the police station too long. A couple of minutes later the sergeant joined us in the car. He sat in front of me in the passenger seat and told his PC to get going and we started driving.

There was quite a lot of traffic, with it being rush hour, so we must have been in the car for about twenty minutes, half an hour, something like that, and we hadn't got that far. We'd stopped at some red lights when someone walked up to the car on the passenger side where the sergeant was sat. It was an oriental man, I don't know where from exactly, but he was carrying his phone and had a baseball cap on that said 'I HEART LONDON', so I figured he was a tourist. He knocked on the window and the sergeant wound the window down and told him they were busy. The tourist said 'I just need to know...' before the sergeant started winding the window up. The sergeant turned to the driver and laughed saying 'Bloody tourists!'

Next thing I know, the tourist punched straight

through the window with both hands. Glass smashed everywhere, and he grabbed the sergeant by the neck, pulling his head towards the broken window. The tourist was shouting 'I need to know where the girl is! I need to know where the girl is!' The sergeant just shouted 'Drive!' and the PC drove straight through the red light, turning right onto a wider road. He put his sirens on and cars started moving out of the way. I turned to look and the Tourist was running after us, running through the traffic as we tried to get away. He had blood pouring down both his arms.

I heard the driver call for back up on his radio and he managed to drive, quite expertly I might add, through the streets, taking some sharp lefts and rights until the Tourist wasn't behind us anymore. He pulled over to check on his sergeant who I think had some blood coming from his nose, but was otherwise OK. The sergeant just told him to 'Get to the nick' saying he'd clean himself up there.

The PC drove on again and turned on to a bit of road that was less busy, where he could finally get some speed up. He kept looking over at his boss, I think he was quite worried about him, when suddenly, out of nowhere a massive German Shepherd dog ran out in the road in front of us and stood barking at the car. The PC swerved to avoid it, going into the opposite lane, and a big white van drove straight into the side of the cars bonnet. The car spun and almost flipped over. The windscreen and the two driver side windows smashed. The van that hit us crashed into a lamp post.

I was dazed, I think I hit my head on the car door, or the window, I'm not really sure, but the two police officers were completely unconscious. I tried to open my door but it must have been either child locked or jammed, so I undid my seatbelt and climbed headfirst out of the broken window on the other side. I think that's when my trousers got ripped. I fell out of the car onto the floor and I guess that's how I got the scrapes on my arm and face."

Yuri paused to take a big sip of hot tea, the cup trembling slightly in his shaky hand.

"I checked the driver's pulse," he continued, "and thankfully he was still alive, just unconscious. The handcuff key was hanging on a carabiner attached to the front of his uniform so I took that and got the handcuffs off. I was worried you'd be stuck in the corridor and that you didn't know how to get out. I couldn't leave you there. I got the map from the back seat and just as I did, the door of the van opened. A big bald man got out of the driver's seat. There was blood on the top of his head and I could see bits of glass stuck in his face. He started walking over towards me and the police car. That's when he started shouting 'I need to know where the girl is!' As he got closer I saw his eyes. They were completely black," Yuri turned to Naomi and said, "and you know where I've seen that before."

Naomi nodded her head, her sombre expression said all that was needed.

"What did you do?" Gabi asked.

"Well, his eyes locked on to mine and he started running towards me. There was already quite a crowd gathering, and he could see I was holding your map. He shouted 'Give me that!' I tried to use the police car as a barrier but he was younger and faster than me and managed to cut me off. He was standing right in front of me, only about two or three steps away. 'Give me that!' he kept shouting. That's when I did something pretty stupid. I held the map out to him and said 'It's here.' The Van Driver took a couple of steps towards me and I hit him really hard in the face. I don't know if it did anything other than surprise him, but it was enough to give me a moment to run.

I ran through the crowd and into an alley that ran between the buildings. I ran until I was sure I wasn't being followed and then I hid until it started getting dark. Once it felt safe enough I made my way back to the tunnel where I found you and brought you back here."

He finished his story and they sat quietly for a few minutes until Naomi broke the silence. "I wonder if the car crash is on the news?"

To Gabi's surprise she reached into her pocket and pulled out the latest iPhone, unlocked it and started scrolling with her index finger. "Yes, dear," Naomi said with a wink in Gabi's direction," I know how to use technology! Ah, here it is… Oh my goodness!"

She turned the phone towards them and showed them a report on the BBC news app:

"PENSIONER PRISONER ESCAPES POLICE

At approximately 6.30 pm this afternoon, a police vehicle was involved in a collision with a van, resulting in two officers being injured. Viral footage taken by bystanders shows an elderly prisoner escaping from the rear of the police car before punching the driver of the van they had collided with, knocking him unconscious. The prisoner then fled the scene. We have contacted the City of London Police for comment, and have been told 'enquiries are ongoing'. More to follow."

Beneath the report was a video clip. Naomi pressed the "PLAY" button in the centre of the clip.

The shaky footage showed Yuri climbing from the police car exactly as he had described. It showed him reaching into the front of the car then taking the handcuffs off. But what happened next shocked her to her core.

As the van driver approached him, she watched Yuri hold out the map. Gabi watched as Yuri then punched the driver in the face and run. The driver flew off camera and the footage followed, showing him slumped against the side of the van. The footage then glitched as the person filming spun back to where Yuri had been standing but he was long gone.

"What the actual f-" Gabi stopped herself from swearing in front of the two elderly strangers, then turned to Yuri, "You have a lot more explaining to do!"

CHAPTER THIRTY-ONE

"I'm not sure now's the time," Yuri said, "it's getting late and you've had a particularly eventful day."

"I'm fine," Gabi replied, "and do you really think I'll be able to sleep knowing I'm in a house with an old man who can do that? How do I know you're not one of them?"

"She's right," Naomi added, "you should probably tell her. At least tell her enough that she isn't worried anymore."

Yuri paused, nodding his head gently as if gathering his thoughts. "Ok," he said, reaching for a book from the bookshelf behind him, "I'm definitely not one of *them*."

He placed the well-worn leather-bound book on the table and opened it up near the front and started reading:

"So God drove out the man; and he placed at the east of the garden of Eden an angel, and a flaming sword which turned every way, to guard the way to the tree of life," Yuri closed the Bible, "Recognise the passage?"

"I don't know it very well but I know the story," Gabi replied, "especially now."

"Well, I haven't always been an old man. My story starts a long time ago. When God created humanity, two people were chosen to live a perfect life. God wanted to see if humans would love him the way the angels did, so he gave them everything they needed. God didn't want people to worship him just in hope of getting something in return. He didn't want humans to love him just when things got hard or when they needed something. So he put them in the Garden, where everything they could need was provided.

They had food, and shelter, and companionship. They had a sense of purpose, and a sense of belonging. They had friendship, and they had each other. But God needed to know they would love him enough to never betray him, how else could he truly measure their love. So he planted a tree, in the Garden. The tree bore fruit unlike any other, for the fruit of that tree would show them a world beyond the garden. It would show them the real world, with all the good, and all the bad. It would give them knowledge of everything they did not have. It would destroy any opportunity of loving God just for love, after all, if they were to eat that fruit they would know God did not control everything in the world. It would show them God had relinquished power and couldn't, *or wouldn't*, help. It would show them they would have to fight to make things right themselves.

The knowledge of Good and Evil is both freeing and debilitating. And God loved those two humans more than anyone else. They were his favourite. And for years Adem and Iv lived happily in perfect harmony with God.

But you know how the story ends. Eventually they both grew tired and bored of their life, craving something different, something more, so Lucifer, who had been God's favourite angel, in his jealousy convinced them to eat the fruit and their eyes were opened.

God's anger was immense. He cast out Lucifer, along with any of the angels that rallied around him. Adem and Iv threw themselves at God's feet, begging for his forgiveness, but he showed them no mercy. He threw them out into the world outside the garden. A world where the ground was hard and dry, where plants struggled to grow, where they would have to rely on each other and on their own abilities to survive.

And then, to ensure they could never return, God hid the garden, and placed a guard at the gate. He gave the guard a sword of flame that could destroy human and angel alike.

That Angel guard, one of the 'Cherubim' was named Uriel. But I go by Yuri now."

"What? You were the guard?" Gabi asked.

"Like I said, I haven't always been this old!"

"What happened?"

"Well, I stood guard at the gate of the Garden for many generations. And no human ever came to the gate. On a few occasions I had to fight a couple of rogue followers of Lucifer's, but it was nothing I couldn't handle. In the end I was stood guarding a hidden entrance to a secret garden that people had long stopped seeking. Away from the comforts of my home, I was made to stand, awake, alone, through the cold of winter and the heat of summer, the sword of flames always at my side, always ready.

Meanwhile, away from the garden, Adem and Iv were living what would now be considered 'normal' life. They were working the ground, building shelters, having children, and growing old. They had a son called Cain, who had children himself, and those children had children, and eventually one of his descendants named Lamech took on two wives. One of them was called Zillah. Zillah gave birth to a baby girl and named her Naamah.

I met her when she was twenty years old. I was stood guard at the garden gate when this young woman appeared. She was petite, with long chestnut hair and dark brown eyes. She was humming a tune to herself, oblivious to anything and anyone else. There was a lightness about her that filled me with joy. She seemed surprised to see me, just as I was to see her, and then she smiled and my heart skipped a beat - or ten…"

"I was only out for a walk!" Naomi added, "I wasn't really paying attention to where I was going…" She gave Gabi a wink and flashed that same wide smile, "It was definitely a good thing."

Before Gabi could say anything, Yuri continued:

"Anyway, Na smiled at me, asked me my name, and we started talking. From that day on she visited me every day. She'd bring me fruit from the trees in her father's orchard. She'd bring her pet dog, Abdi, to see me. She would tell me stories about her life and, slowly but surely, I found I couldn't live without her."

"And I couldn't live without him," Naomi reached across the table and took Yuri's hand.

"But we couldn't live at the gate of the garden," Yuri continued, "So I had a choice to make. I pleaded with God to allow me to leave, but he wouldn't hear of it, so one day I decided to do something I thought I would never do - I chose to leave my post.

I turned my back on my orders and used the sword forged in the fires of Heaven to bring down an avalanche of rocks, crushing the entrance to the Garden, sealing it forever beneath a mountain of stones. It was around that time that Gabriel sought me out. He found me and asked to borrow the sword. He said another faction of angels had turned against God and he needed to stop them. I guess it was Damriel and his army, but I didn't care. I took a jewel from the hilt, to ensure he returned the true sword to me, then I handed it over. I told him to keep it safe and then I returned to my beloved Naamah."

"What did God do after you left your post?" Gabi asked.

"He was less than pleased…" Yuri laughed, "definitely less than pleased."

Yuri paused again to put the old Bible back on the shelf and rubbed his eyes. "I'm getting tired," he said, "Can I finish the story in the morning?"

"I guess," Gabi said, yawning, "I'm pretty tired too…"

"Come," Naomi said, "I'll show you to your room."

Gabi followed Naomi out the kitchen and up the stairs. "The bathroom's straight ahead," Naomi told her as they reached the top of the stairs, "and this is your room."

She took Gabi into a room to the right of the bathroom. It was a medium sized room with a single bed next to a window. There was a desk in one corner and more books on shelves above the bed and along the wall opposite the bed. It was cozy and welcoming.

"I'll bring you some towels. Feel free to have a bath or a shower, either now or in the morning."

"Thank you," Gabi replied, "you've been so kind."

"It's the least we can do," Naomi replied, "You're carrying a lot of responsibility for someone so young. We just want to help."

Naomi turned to walk out the room and Gabi asked: "Was it really you, all those years ago?"

"Yes, it was. And we'll tell you all about it in the morning, but right now, you need to sleep. Good night, Gabi. I'll leave the towels outside your door."

"Good night," Gabi replied, "see you tomorrow."

Naomi closed the door and Gabi lay down on the bed. She pulled the covers around her, closed her eyes and, within seconds, was fast asleep.

Meanwhile, forty miles or so to the south of where Gabi slept, Melchiriel, Rafa, and Harriet were wide awake.

They had been alone from the moment they'd arrived and had checked everywhere their chains allowed for an escape route. Their captors had chained them in such a way that they could not reach the only visible door, which was undoubtedly locked. And now night had fallen, the room was pitch black.

"It's been a long time, old friend," Damriel's instantly recognisable voice cut through the darkness like a scalpel, "A very long time."

"Not long enough," Harriet heard Melchiriel reply, "and I am not your friend."

"Really? I guess you've forgotten the fun we had in Magdala? The parties we went to together in Betar? I remember you used to be the life of the party. What happened?"

"I am *not* your friend, Damriel."

"That's not what *He* believes, is it? And *He* knew you best of all…"

Melchiriel didn't answer.

Damriel spoke again: "*He* never trusted you again, did he? *He* knows you, like I know you. *He* knows what you're truly like. Children," he said, turning his attention to Harriet and Rafa, "you can't trust anything he tells you. Your friend Melchiriel's a fallen angel, just like the rest of us. He's just using you to earn his way back to Heaven. And I can't be having that."

The darkness became darker as shadows filled the room, pouring over Rafa and Harriet like a rushing river, invading every pore, filling their very souls with anguish. Harriet screamed as her body convulsed in agony. This was a feeling she had never experienced before. Her body felt as though it had been emptied of all hope, all joy, all love. Instead she was filled with a loneliness she had never felt, as though she were detached from all humanity, from any hope of freedom. She could see nothing but the dark as demonic voices filled her head:

"Shut up!"

"You're worthless."

"You're nothing."

"No one cares."

"No one loves you."

"They're all laughing at you."

"You're dead now."

"With us now."

"Just give up."

"You've got nothing to live for."

She writhed in pain on the floor next to Rafa, tears streaming down her face as she cried out into the darkness, hour after hour, as all hope, and all solace, for her, faded from existence.

There was no rest, as invisible blades sliced and scoured their souls, peeling them away from their body like skin being peeled from a carcass revealing nothing but live flesh on which the salt of sadness, despair, and endless loneliness, was poured.

At daybreak Damriel returned. "Leave them," he said.

Immediately Harriet's pain stopped. In the half-light of their prison she could see Rafa lying on his side, his breathing shallow, his face pale. The light and life she normally saw in his eyes was all but gone.

"Where is she, little girl?" Damriel asked. His voice was soft and gentle. "Where is she?"

"I don't know," Harriet replied, "and even if I did I wouldn't tell you."

"Do you want your suffering to continue?" Damriel asked, "Do you really want more?"

"No," Harriet whispered, "I don't."

"THEN TELL ME WHERE SHE IS!" Damriel roared. His right hand shot out, grabbing her by the throat. He lifted her off the floor. "TELL ME WHERE SHE IS!" he screamed. His fingers tightened their grip and Harriet gasped for air; "I... can't... br-"

"Let her go!" Rafa shouted. Damriel turned just in time to see a large hard back book flying straight at him. It struck him right between the eyes.

"Let her go!" Rafa shouted again, picking up another volume from the dusty stack of books in the corner next to where he was chained. With a swing of his arm, the book flew from his hand, straight towards the demon's face.

Damriel dropped Harriet and batted the book out of the air. He crossed the room in a flash, and picked Rafa up by his hair, lifting him off the ground as if he were a rag doll.

"That was stupid," he spat, "you think you're a hero?"

"No," Rafa stammered, "but at least I'm not a bully…"

"I need nothing more from you," Damriel said and with a flick of his wrist he threw Rafa aside. The chains around Rafa's feet tightened bringing his body crashing to the ground. His head hit the hard floor with a thud, and his body lay still.

Damriel stormed out, slamming the door behind him.

"Are you OK?" Harriet asked, "Rafa, are you ok?"

Rafa didn't reply.

He felt no more pain as he breathed out one last time. And then there was silence.

CHAPTER THIRTY-TWO

Gabi woke up. She rubbed her eyes and looked over at the clock on the wall. It was just after nine in the morning. She jumped out of bed and pulled on her trousers just as there was a knock on the door. "Come in!" Gabi said smiling as Naomi put her head round the door.

"Morning Gabi, would you like some breakfast? It's all ready."

"I'll be right down," She was feeling hungry again.

After going to the bathroom and washing her face she felt a little more awake and went downstairs. She sat in the same chair she had sat in the night before, opposite Yuri who was already tucking in to his second boiled egg, dipping toast soldiers in the runny yolk.

"Morning Gabi," he said, looking up, his mouth full, "how did you sleep?"

"Really well actually," Gabi said, "I was clearly tired…"

"You looked tired last night," Yuri said, wiping his face with a white cloth serviette, "hopefully today will be less 'busy'," He emphasised the word *busy* doing quotation marks with his fingers in the air.

Gabi laughed; "Not much hope of that. I've got to find the sword today."

"Don't worry. I'll help you as much as I can. I obviously can't go back to the shop. They'll be looking for me there…"

Gabi felt a sense of relief wash over her. She hadn't realised how worried she'd been about having to find the sword on her own.

"Before we go, can you finish telling me what happened after you left your post as Guardian of the Garden?"

"Of course," Yuri smiled, the wrinkles around his eyes deepening as he did, "now, where was I?"

"You had given the sword up to Gabriel and returned to Naamah, but I don't know what happened after that. You said God was angry."

"Oh yes," Yuri said, "and that's an understatement! I came back after burying the entrance to the garden under the mountain of rocks, and I went to find my Na. She was outside her parents' house, looking after her nieces and nephews. They were kicking some sort of wooden ball around.

I remember her face when she saw me walking up the road. At first, she was shocked as she had never seen me away from my post. Then her whole face lit up with this enormous smile. Everything about her filled me with joy. And still does." He paused, looking over at Naomi who was busy making a jug of coffee in the kitchen.

"When she saw me," he continued, "she ran towards me, threw her arms around me and held me so tight I could hardly breathe! She kept repeating 'You're here! You're here!' and from that day on we have never been apart.

It took some weeks before God noticed I wasn't at my post. I guess I'd been there so long, he didn't need to keep checking. Or he just wasn't that interested. I had started working for Na's father, looking after the animals, and helping him manage his crops, and before long Na and I were engaged and were soon to be married.

It was on our wedding day that things took a turn for the worse. We were getting married in Na's father's vineyard. Everything was set up beautifully. The *chuppah*, that's the raised canopy we stood under for the ceremony, was decorated with vines from the vineyard. The delicate white flowers breaking up the green of the vine blended in to the beautiful blue skies. Standing there, in that moment, I couldn't tell where Earth ended and Heaven began. Everything was perfect.

As part of the *Kiddushin*, the betrothal ceremony, I didn't have a traditional ring to give Naamah. Instead I gave her a gold necklace on which I had hung that single jewel I'd taken from the hilt of the Sword of Flames."

Instinctively Gabi reached for the pendant hanging around her own neck. "Has she still got it?" she asked.

"I'm getting to that," Yuri replied. He poured himself a cup of tea from the teapot and continued: "I placed the pendant around her neck. I also handed her a contract of marriage, my *ketubah*. In this I promised to love, honour, and cherish her, to be faithful to her, and to love her with all my heart, mind and soul, remaining by her side for all eternity. Naamah signed the contract, promising the same. The rabbi blessed the contract and prayed over us.

As part of the wedding ceremony we drank wine at certain points, the wine, of course, came from her father's grapes. As tradition demands, the ceremony is concluded with the groom breaking two glasses. It's important to remember sadness, even at the most joyful of times. I always found this a strange tradition of ours, until someone once told me that if there were no shadows we would forget the sun.

I had just placed the glasses on the floor under a cloth, ready to crush them with my right foot when suddenly everything went dark. Black storm clouds filled the sky, covering the sun. A mighty wind whipped around us, tearing the *chuppah* away. The priest, along with most of the guests ran to take cover, leaving Naamah and me exposed on the raised platform. Lightning struck the vines in the fields around us and the whole harvest burst into flames.

Without warning, the wind suddenly stopped, and there was silence. All I could hear was the gentle crackle of flames as the burning grapevines cast an eerie, flickering light on Naamah's face. I pulled her close, wrapping my arms around her to keep her safe. That was when I heard *his* voice. The voice of God. And he was angry. He was so angry.

'WHAT HAVE YOU DONE?' His voice filled my head until there was nothing but him and me. 'WHAT HAVE YOU DONE?'

'I've done nothing wrong,' I told him.

'YOU LEFT YOUR POST. YOU DISOBEYED ME. THERE WILL BE CONSEQUENCES FOR YOUR SIN.'

'I'll take any punishment,' I told him, 'but do not hurt Naamah. She's innocent and I love her.'

'YOU LOVE HER MORE THAN YOU LOVE ME. THIS IS YOUR GREATEST SIN. AND FOR THAT YOU ARE CURSED. YOU WILL WANDER THE EARTH, ALONE FOR AN ETERNITY, YOU WILL AGE SLOWLY UNTIL EVENTUALLY YOU ARE TOO FRAIL TO LIVE A NORMAL LIFE. YOU WILL CRAVE DEATH AND IT WILL NOT COME. YOU WILL NOT HAVE CHILDREN TO CARE FOR YOU. INSTEAD YOU WILL WATCH ALL THOSE YOU LOVE DIE AROUND YOU.'

It was then I heard Naamah's voice cutting through the darkness like a silver ray of light: 'You can't make him do this alone. We signed a contract that we would spend eternity together. A contract we signed in *your* name.'

'THE CONTRACT MAY BE SIGNED, BUT THE CEREMONY IS NOT COMPLETE. YOU ARE NOT YET BOUND TOGETHER.'

At this I heard the sound of glass breaking as Naamah crushed the glasses under her feet.

'It is now.' she said.

There was silence for a moment. And then God's voice, tinged with sadness, and as gentle as the murmur of a running stream said: 'So be it. You have chosen your path. You are bound to his same fate, his same suffering.'

'And his same love,' I heard her whisper.

As suddenly as it had arrived, the darkness faded, giving way to sunlight and blue skies again. Around us the scorched vineyard and scattered decorations were all that remained as evidence that God himself had attended our wedding.

Naamah's father came out of the storehouse he had taken shelter in and saw what had happened to his crops. 'I'm a ruined man,' he said, 'and it's all your fault. You have brought down the wrath of God on me and my family. You are no longer welcome here.'

With that his brothers and their children surrounded us and chased us off his land.

We wandered for many months, taking jobs wherever we could to buy food and shelter, until we eventually found a home far away from her family, in the south of what you call Israel now.

We found ourselves having to move every ten years or so, rebuilding and restarting, with new names, and new homes, and new friends. It's hard to pretend you're 'normal' when after ten years you show no sign of ageing as grey hairs and wrinkles start to show on all your friends."

There was a sadness in his eyes, as though he were remembering all the people, all the friends, he had lost. Gabi reached out and took the old man's hands in hers: "Did you ever have children?"

"No," he replied, "God cursed us to be alone, cursed us to never have children of our own. But there was Rosalie."

Naomi sat down on the chair next to Gabi and said: "She was like a daughter to us."

"Yes, she was," Yuri said.

Naomi continued: "We were living in the south of

France in the early 1600s, in Marseille. Yuri was working as a dock hand, helping load and unload ships that came to the port. I didn't have any work at the time, but we were alright. We had always been careful with money, saving enough to make sure we were always provided for, without drawing attention to ourselves.

One day Yuri was came home carrying a baby girl. She can't have been more than a couple of weeks old. He'd found her, abandoned on a pile of old sails left to rot outside one of the warehouses where they stored shipping supplies. There was no one around. No note. Nothing to indicate where she had come from. He couldn't leave her there. And there was no way I could abandon her to the elements again. We took her in and named her Rosalie. And she was so beautiful. And so kind. And so loving.

We moved shortly after that, as people were asking questions about how I had had a baby without appearing to be pregnant. I told people she was my niece, that my sister had suddenly died and had no one to care for her, but I don't think many people believed me. So we moved to Calais. It was another port town, so we knew Yuri would be able to get work there. Calais had been owned by the British for almost 400 years or so until the late 1500s, so there were still a lot of British people living there.

Rosalie grew up and we stayed in Calais probably the longest we had ever stayed anywhere. We were there for almost twenty years. When she was 19 years old she met this young Englishman called William. He was as kind and as caring as she was and it wasn't long before they got married.

I gave her my pendant on her wedding day for she was as close to a real daughter as I would ever have. They sailed to London two days after their wedding as William had a new job at the bank his father worked at.

We moved shortly after, heading to Lille, that was still under the control of the Belgians, or maybe it was the Spanish at the time, I can't remember. But it was like being in a different country which meant a brand new start for us."

"What happened to Rosalie?" Gabi asked.

"Sadly, she died a few years later. She had written to tell me she had had a baby - a girl she had named Hannah and we were planning on visiting her. But two weeks later we received a letter from William. Rosalie had been trampled by a runaway horse and carriage outside their house in the City of London. She had died instantly. We moved on. We couldn't burden William, or baby Hannah, with our secret so we cut contact. I never saw William again. And I never met Hannah. It's still my only regret."

A single tear rolled down Naomi's cheek.

"I'm so sorry," Gabi said, "that must have been so hard."

"It was. But we made the choice and had to live with it. And at least we had each other."

"We've always had each other," Yuri added.

The three sat together in silence for a few moments before Naomi said: "Shall I make you another cup of tea before you head out?"

She got up from the table and walked over to the kitchen.

"The way you took Rosalie in as your own is incredible," Gabi said, "She definitely knew she was loved. It's strange how much her story is like mine though. I was adopted too, and all I have left of my mum is this necklace she gave me."

With that she pulled her necklace out from under her t-shirt and Yuri gasped: "That's Na's necklace! That's the one she gave Rosalie! It's the one I made!"

CHAPTER THIRTY-THREE

Gabi was stunned.

"Are you saying this jewel is from the Sword of Flames? The one I've been looking for?" she asked.

"Absolutely.' Yuri said, his eyes suddenly moist, "I'd recognise it anywhere."

"May I?" Naomi was standing next to Gabi, trembling slightly.

"Of course!" Gabi reached to unclasp the necklace.

"No, leave it on," Naomi said, stopping her, "That necklace protects you from the shadows. While you wear it they can't touch you. They can't invade your body, or take over your mind. I just want to hold it one more time."

Gabi leaned forward as Naomi gently reached out and held the pendant in her right hand. Gabi saw Naomi smile as tears formed in the corner of the gentle woman's eyes. "I never thought I'd see this again," Naomi said, "it means you must be related to Rosalie! That makes you more than just a friend. You're family!"

Gabi suddenly found herself being held firm in Naomi's arms in an embrace that somehow felt like home. She wrapped her arms around Naomi and returned the hug overcome by emotion. For a moment time stood still as she finally felt like she belonged again.

"We better get on with finding this sword." Yuri's voice brought Gabi back to reality, "Now, where did you say it was? St Paul's?"

"I think so," Gabi replied, drying her eyes, "my however many great-grandfather's book said it was in *'the most sacred place in England's primary capital cathedral'*, so I guess that means St Paul's cathedral…"

"You'll be pleased to hear that's not far from here," Yuri said, "less than a mile in fact."

"Shall we get going then?" Gabi asked, "The sooner we get this, the sooner I can help Rafa, Harriet, and Melc."

"Of course."

Gabi put her shoes on, picked up her bag, carefully put the school plans in the bag's front section, and waited patiently as Yuri put on a light coat. She noticed he also selected a hat from a hook at the bottom of the stairs. It was one of those cloth hats with a fairly wide brim that a lot of old men seem to wear in the summer.

"Just minimising the chances of being recognised," Yuri said, "now that that video is doing the rounds…"

"Good idea."

Gabi opened the door and stepped out into the morning sun. It was a beautiful spring day, not a cloud in the sky and the temperature was just below 20°C. They turned left out of the courtyard and joined the busy street. There were many people out and about that morning, and no one seemed to look twice at what they must have assumed was just another grandfather showing his grand-daughter around the City's tourist sights.

Having walked for about ten minutes, along Fleet Street, they had just crossed a busy crossing by an underground station when Gabi heard a commotion. About fifteen feet behind them a dog walker seemed to be struggling with the dogs she was walking. The dog walker must have been in her early twenties. She was slim, with long brown hair and was wearing a zipped-up hoodie with a picture of a paw print on the left-hand side. She had four dogs on leads and one of them, a large German Shepherd, was snarling and pulling at the lead. The dog-walker was shouting "Stop it, Fenrir! Sit! Calm down!" but the dog was pulling harder and harder on the lead.

The dog was clearly looking in Gabi's direction. "This doesn't feel right!" she said, grabbing Yuri's arm.

Yuri took one look at the dog and shouted: "Run, Gabi, run!" Gabi broke into a sprint dragging Yuri with her, just as the German Shepherd broke free from its lead and sprinted after them, barking and foaming at the mouth.

They ran across the road into Cathedral Place, and as they did Gabi heard the screeching of breaks and a loud yelp. She turned to see the dog had been hit by a police van and was now lying motionless on the road. Three police officers got out of the van and walked towards the dog.

As they approached Gabi saw the dog's eyes open. They were completely black. No pupils. No movement. The dead eyes of a dog possessed. She watched as one of the officers put his hand out towards the fallen dog. The dog suddenly reared its head, grabbed the man's hand in his mouth and shook it. Blood started pouring out the sides of the dog's snarling mouth as it bounded across the road towards them. Gabi turned and ran up the stairs into the cathedral, grabbing Yuri on the way, the dog only metres behind her.

They had just crossed the threshold as the dog ran at full speed towards the open door of St Paul's Cathedral. It squealed as it ran into an invisible wall, its head snapped backwards with a loud crack. The dog lay motionless for a second time just outside the cathedral door, its neck broken. This time it would not get up again.

"What was that?" Gabi asked.

"One of Damriel's army," Yuri replied, "they can't enter places of worship while they're possessing people, and they can't possess anyone once they're inside. If that dog's dead then the Shadow inside it has died too."

A crowd started gathering around the dead dog's corpse leaving the cathedral almost empty.

"Now's our chance," Yuri said, "While they're all busy with that, we can look for the sword."

Gabi turned and started heading towards the altar at the far end of the magnificent cathedral. She had never been inside St Paul's before and the sheer size of the place took her completely by surprise. It was unexpectedly beautiful. The cathedral's cavernous nave stretched out before her, its high vaulted ceilings seemingly reaching up to the heavens, the floor decorated in alternating black and white stones, like a giant chess board. The polished marble columns lining the nave, elegant and simple, glinted in the mid-morning sunlight streaming through the stained-glass windows.

Despite the adrenaline still coursing through her veins, Gabi felt a peaceful stillness envelop her as she took in the delicate carvings on the pulpit and the graceful curves of the altar. She paused as she reached the heart of the cathedral, taking it all in. High above her head, she could see the Whispering Gallery – St Paul's famous domed roof, built in such a way that you could whisper at one end of the gallery and be heard clearly at the other.

"Come on," Yuri said, in a hushed voice, "We've got to find the sword."

Gabi snapped back to reality and followed Yuri to the altar.

The high altar was made of white marble, decorated with gold detailing. Giant pillars supported an ornate roof of wood and gold on which a pair of sculptured angels seemed to be standing guard.

"Know them?" Gabi asked Yuri, smiling.

"Ha!" he laughed, "That's the first time I've heard you joke since we met yesterday. It's good. And no, I don't know them!"

"Where do you think it's hidden?" Gabi asked.

"I don't know, I guess around the back here."

They stepped over the rope that hung across the aisle to dissuade visitors from getting any closer, and quietly walked around the back of the altar.

Yuri stood watch while Gabi felt around the back of the altar. She ran her fingers along every edge, feeling for any hidden button or catch she could find. She checked along every gold detail, every raised edge, but found nothing. At the base of the large gold cross that sat atop the altar, was a painted image of a lamb. Gabi pressed both her thumbs into the centre of the image, hoping this would release something when a loud voice interrupted her:

"What are you doing? Get your hands off!" An angry looking priest was running up the aisle towards them. He was wearing a light blue shirt with a white dog collar under a black blazer. His highly polished shoes made a tapping noise on the marble floor as he hurried towards them.

Gabi released the cross and took a step back. "I'm sorry," she said, "I was only looking…"

"Why are you up here?" the priest asked, "It's clearly off limits."

"I'm really sorry," Gabi said again, "I'm doing a history project about St Paul's so my grandad brought me here. I read in one of my books that there's a secret hidden at the heart of the cathedral and I was just trying to find it…"

"A secret?" the priest replied, "I've never heard of that, but this isn't the heart of the Cathedral. That's over there." He pointed to a large star carved into the floor directly below the dome, right in the centre of where the two wings of the temple intersected the nave.

"Thank you, Mr…?"

"It's Reverend Fry," the priest replied, softening a little, "but you can call me Logan, everyone else does. Now, what's this secret?"

"I'm not exactly sure what I'm looking for," Gabi lied, "but I'm sure I'll know when I see it."

Gabi walked over to the star design embedded in the floor tiles. It was about 20-foot-wide and looked like the star she'd seen on old maps denoting compass points. Each point of the star was a long thin triangle in alternating black and red.

In the centre of the star was a circular bronze grate, around which a Latin inscription read:

"Subtus conditur huius ecclesiae et urbis conditor Christophorus Wren qui visit annos ultra nonaginta non sibi sed bono publico lector si monumentum requiris circumspice obiit XXV feb aetatis XCI an MDCCXXIII"

"This celebrates the life of Christopher Wren, who designed the Cathedral," Logan said in a hushed voice, "this is his final resting place. The inscription says 'Here lies Christopher Wren, the founder of this church and this city, who lived over ninety years, not for himself but for the good of the public. If you are seeking his monument, look around you. He died on February 25 1723 aged 91.' He is the very heart of the cathedral. It was his passion, his eye for beauty, and his love for God and this city that brought the cathedral to life."

"It must be in there," Gabi said, "The dates tie in, and everything fits. It's got to be hidden in there."

"There's no way in to the tomb," Logan said, "It's been sealed since 1723. Where exactly did you find out about this so-called secret?"

"It was in a book," Gabi said, choosing her words carefully, "from 1787. It said it was hidden in 'the most sacred place in the heart of England's primary capital cathedral.'"

"That can only mean here," Yuri added.

"Unless the author wanted to tell the truth but obfuscate its meaning…" Logan said.

"What do you mean?" Gabi asked.

"St Paul's is definitely London's primary, most important cathedral," he said, "but, if the author meant England's primary capital city, primary of course meaning 'first', then you're in the wrong city altogether. Winchester was the first capital city of England, named the capital by King Alfred in about 871CE."

"So we might be looking in exactly the wrong place?" Gabi said.

"I think you might be."

Gabi's heart sank. It felt like Rafa was now even further away. She sank to the floor, tears forming in the corners of her eyes.

"This is really important to you, isn't it?" Logan said gently, "It's clearly not just a school project."

Yuri moved to Gabi's side, a little more defensively than may have been necessary. "We can't tell you any more than that," Yuri said, before adding, "Sorry."

"I understand," Logan said, holding out a packet of tissues he had taken from his trouser pocket, "We all have secrets. We all have things we feel we can't tell others. But tell me this: whatever you're trying to find, is it for you, or for someone else?"

Gabi took a tissue out and dried her eyes, "I need it to help my cousin, and my friends. I didn't want any of this in the first place."

"I thought you'd say that. Let me help." Logan pulled a phone from his pocket and typed something. "I've just told my boss I'm going to be busy this afternoon with some urgent pastoral work… So, do you want a lift to Winchester?"

CHAPTER THIRTY-FOUR

Gabi looked at Yuri. He shrugged. "Can we trust him?" she whispered.

"I think so," came the reply, "but we've got no other way of getting there. If we go out in the open I'll either be recognised because of that news clip, or we'll be found by more shadow soldiers."

"Yeah, I guess…"

"Plus," Yuri continued, "I'd rather take my chances with one person, than any number of people out in the city."

"You're right," Gabi said, turning to follow Logan towards a small door at the far end of the building, "I'm just being careful."

Logan's car was parked in a small car park at the back of the cathedral. There were signs up telling visitors that this was a staff car park and that any vehicle parked there without a permit was likely to get a parking ticket. It was a plain looking metallic grey Honda Civic. Gabi walked to the back door as Yuri had already opened the front passenger door.

"The handle's at the top," Logan said, "sort of on the side."

"Thanks. How far is it to Winchester Cathedral?"

"It should take just under a couple of hours,

depending on traffic," he replied, opening the driver's door, "Don't tell anyone, but I've done it in just over an hour and half before. Although as a priest I probably shouldn't confess to speeding!"

Gabi sat down in the back behind Yuri and put her seatbelt on.

They sat in silence as Logan drove them through the city. Gabi rested her head against the window, letting the sights of the busy streets of London rush past her. She allowed herself to relax and, as the adrenaline slowly wore away, she found herself drifting off.

When she opened her eyes again they were on the motorway. Logan and Yuri were talking quite animatedly in the front, laughing together as though there were old friends.

"Hey sleepy head!" Logan said, catching her eyes in the rearview mirror, "Good nap?"

Gabi ignored his questions. "How long was I asleep for?" she asked.

"Just under an hour," he replied, "we're on the M3 motorway, about halfway now. We were just saying we'll probably stop to get some lunch at the Services in Fleet. You ok with that?"

She hadn't realised quite how hungry she was. "That sounds good," she said, "as long as we can still get to Winchester in time."

"It'll be fine. Plenty of time," Logan replied.

It wasn't long before Gabi saw the turn off for Fleet Services. The big sign at the slip road advertising Burger King, Pizza Express, and Subway. As they pulled into the busy car park, Logan said: "That's definitely weird…"

"What is?" Yuri asked.

"There's a white Toyota people carrier that's been behind us pretty much since we left London. I don't know if it's following us, but it's pulled in behind us."

"Why do you think they're following us?" Gabi asked.

"They've kept the same speed, speeding up as I've

sped up, slowing down when I slowed down. And always keeping two or three cars behind."

Gabi turned around to see where they were. The car pulled into a parking space three rows behind them and the occupants got out. The driver was a middle-aged man in his late forties. He looked like a typical dad; a little overweight, his hair was greying around the edges and he had a salt and pepper beard. He was wearing a baggy black hoody and jeans.

His wife was shorter, slim and had her hair scraped back in a tight pony tail. Their two teenage children got out the back. Both taller than their parents, they looked like they might be twins, although they were wearing completely different clothes. One had a Slipknot hoody and very baggy jeans, a thin metal chain looping from his waist to his back pocket. His jet-black hair was longer and swept across his face.

His brother, on the other hand, was wearing a matching Adidas tracksuit in emerald green with three white stripes down the sides of his arms and legs. He was carrying a tiny 'man bag' and wearing bright white Nike trainers. His hair, shaved to a grade one, was bright blonde.

Gabi watched as the family walked, laughing, towards the doors of the Services Concourse where all the shops were. They looked like a fairly normal family. "I don't think they are following us," she said, "they're not even looking to see if we go in behind them."

"You might be right," Logan said, "Come on. Let's grab something to eat quickly and get back on the road."

They walked through the glass doors into the giant food hall. It was about the size of a football pitch with a domed glass roof. There were tables and chairs dotted around the middle of the concourse with different eating outlets all around the outside. Gabi could see a Subway, a Burger King, a KFC, a Chinese Noodle place, a Pizza Express, and of course a WHSmith.

They made their way to Subway where Gabi ordered

her favourite sandwich, a six-inch chicken bacon ranch, with lettuce, tomatoes, and Chipotle Southwest sauce. She looked around while she waited for Logan and Yuri. The family from the Toyota were nowhere to be seen.

After a quick visit to the toilets, they walked back to the car. The white car was gone. "I guess they weren't following us after all," Logan said, "maybe I'm just being a bit paranoid…"

"We must be fairly close to Winchester now, aren't we?" Yuri asked.

"Yeah, about half an hour or so and we'll be there," Logan said.

Gabi settled back into the car and put her seat belt on as they rejoined the motorway, traveling south. The motorway was fairly busy which wasn't unexpected for this time of day. Gabi noticed that Logan seemed to enjoy driving in the middle lane, just above the speed limit. Not enough to get stopped by the police, but enough to be driving a little faster than most of the cars in the "slow" lane. They had just passed the exit for Basingstoke when she saw it. The white Toyota was on their left as Logan casually drove past it.

The dad was driving and laughing. He was gesticulating with his hands as he talked and his wife was laughing. The twins, sat in the back, didn't seem to be involved in the conversation. Emo Twin was staring out the window at the passing countryside while Tracksuit Twin had Apple Airpods in his ears and seemed engrossed in whatever he was watching on his phone screen.

Relaxing a bit, Gabi leaned forward, putting her head between the two front seats and said: "Yeah, we've just gone past that white car again. I think they're just a normal family."

As Gabi focused on the road ahead, Logan indicated left and pulled into the left lane, getting ready to leave the motorway at the next exit. "We're almost there," he said, "next exit and we're practically at the Cathedral."

Less than ten minutes later Logan indicated again and came off the motorway onto the slip road where a big blue sign said "WINCHESTER" and a smaller brown sign indicated they should turn right at the next roundabout for the cathedral.

Two cars behind them, the white Toyota's indicator also turned on as the driver gripped the steering wheel firmly, his eyes fixed on the Honda Civic ahead. Beside him his wife was silent too as she, along with the twins in the back, stared intently at the car Gabi was in.

As the Honda Civic drove past a large Tesco supermarket and a fire station, the White Toyota followed, staying two cars behind. It followed as the Honda drove down the hill and over a little bridge leading into Winchester City Centre, past a homeless shelter and on towards the shops and the Cathedral.

As they drove past the homeless shelter Gabi turned around and looked out the rear windscreen.

"Shit!" she said, "I was wrong. We are being followed!"

She saw Logan's eyes catch hers in the rearview mirror as he looked out the back of the car. "Which one?" he asked.

"The white one," Gabi replied, "It's the same car we saw at the services…"

"OK," Logan replied, his voice calmer than Gabi expected, "I know Winchester quite well. We'll lose them…"

Gabi felt the car speed up as Logan put the car in a lower gear and pressed the accelerator. Behind them the white car followed suit. The Honda Civic hugged the corners of the road like a well-tuned racecar, following the curves of the road into the city centre's one-way system.

The white car had also sped up and was almost catching up with them, now less than a single car's length away. They turned left by a KFC restaurant and round to the right by a McDonald's. Gabi gripped the handle above her door, holding on tight to stop herself being thrown across the car. The little Honda sped up the hill towards a row of pubs and clubs then took a sharp left, a sharp right and sped up towards an old stone monument. Their pursuers pulled into the right-hand lane, pulling alongside them. Gabi could see their blackened eyes staring at her as the driver yanked the wheel to the left, causing the two cars to collide. Sparks flew as Logan countered the force of the impact, steering right to keep the car on the road.

As they approached a mini roundabout, Gabi's whole body was thrown forward in her seat as Logan slammed on the brakes. The white Toyota sped ahead, going straight over the roundabout up the hill. Logan pulled the wheel right and turned, staying on the one-way system, their pursuers heading the wrong way up the hill.

Logan immediately turned right again at a police station into some smaller roads, doubled back on himself, crossed the one-way system they had just been on, and turned left again. A few more short, sharp turns and the white car was nowhere to be seen.

"I think we've lost them," Logan said, "at least for now."

"Let's get to the Cathedral," Yuri said, "we need to get somewhere safe."

Logan stopped the car on a narrow side road at the rear of the Cathedral grounds and the three of them ran across the well-manicured lawn towards the Cathedral doors, only slowing down when they were a few steps away from the entrance.

Standing by the door was a slim, middle aged man. His black cassock and dog collar gave away his priestly profession. The look on his face indicated he wasn't particularly pleased with his role greeting guests.

"Welcome to Winchester Cathedral," he said, in a dull monotone, "One of the oldest Cathedrals in Britain. It was built in…"

"Rupert! It's me!" Logan interrupted.

The priests whole demeanour suddenly changed. His face lit up, as a smile spread from ear to ear.

"Logan!" he exclaimed, "It's been so long!"

"We need to get inside," Logan said, "I'll explain later. Can we skip the tour?"

"I guess," Rupert replied, "I presume you still know your way around?"

"Of course," Logan said.

"The Cathedral closes at six pm. It would be great to meet up after I finish?"

"Bishop on the Bridge at eight?" Logan said.

"Still my favourite pub!" Rupert said, "See you there!"

He smiled and opened a little side door. Gabi, Yuri, and Logan stepped through, bypassing the roped off area where several tourists were waiting to buy their entrance tickets.

"Enjoy the Cathedral," Rupert said, waving, "I'm looking forward to seeing you later!"

He closed the door behind them as Gabi followed Logan and Yuri deeper into the impressive ancient building.

CHAPTER THIRTY-FIVE

Stepping into the Cathedral, Gabi was struck by an overwhelming sense of grandeur. The vast ancient space was filled with the soft glow of stained-glass windows, the colourful patterns they cast creating a tapestry of gentle light on the stone floors and walls. Soaring gothic arches and vaulted ceilings seemed to stretch up to the heavens.

She followed Logan and Yuri down the centre aisle, in awe of the sheer scale of the Cathedral. There was something about this place that seemed to put St Paul's Cathedral to shame. The space seemed to go on forever, with row upon row of carved wooden pews stretching out either side.

At the far end of the building she could see the high altar, bathed in the warm glow of flickering candles. The intricate carvings of angels and saints seemed to come alive in the dancing light, their faces serene and peaceful. Winchester Boys' choir was practising in the stalls beyond the altar, their voices filling the space with hauntingly beautiful harmonies.

Logan dropped back and whispered in her ear: "It's incredible isn't it?"

Gabi nodded. "Yeah…" she said, her voice hushed.

"We should probably get on with finding the sword

though…" Logan added.

Gabi's face dropped. "How do you…" she began to ask.

"Don't worry," Yuri said, interrupting her, "I told him everything on the car journey while you were sleeping. I trust him."

"OK…" Gabi said, but her voice betrayed her doubt about this decision.

"We're looking for the heart of the Cathedral, right?" Logan asked.

"That's what the book said," Gabi replied.

"Traditionally, the heart of any cathedral is the point where the two arms of the building intersect with the main body. It's a symbol of where Christ's heart was when he hung on the cross."

"Right," Gabi said, "just like at St Paul's."

She ran ahead to the point on the centre aisle at the intersection between the arms and the body of the building. There, in the centre of the aisle, was a large white slab of stone, different to all the other stones that made up the cathedral floor. There was nothing written on it. No markings at all. It looked as if it had slowly been worn down by hundreds of years of worshipers' feet walking over it.

"This has got to be it," she said crouching down, ignoring the tourists milling around her. She ran her finger around the edges. There was nothing obvious. No hidden switches or hand holds. Nothing that could be used to lift the giant stone slab.

"What are you doing?" Logan asked, standing next to her.

"There's got to be some secret switch, or a way to get this stone up."

"I don't think so," he said, holding out his hand to her, "But I do think there's another way. Come."

Gabi took hold of his hand as he helped her to her feet.

"This way," he said.

Gabi walked with him as he led her round into one

of the arms of the building.

"When I was newly qualified I spent a lot of time here," he said, "and I loved exploring this building. While I was here I discovered something special in the Holy Sepulchre Chapel…"

He led them to a tiny chapel, off to the side. The ancient entrance was very narrow and the chapel itself was tiny. All over the walls and ceilings were cracked, faded paintings of saints, angels, and Jesus himself.

"These are 12th Century paintings," Logan said, "and this is the one of the oldest parts of the Cathedral. I used to come here when I needed to be alone to pray. It was on one of those occasions that I found this."

The priest walked around the back of the stone altar and knelt down. He ran his right hand along the edge of the altar top until he came to a point almost exactly at the centre. "Here it is," he said.

A cracking sound echoed around the cathedral as a large stone block slid gently into the ground, revealing a dark hole directly under the altar. "It's best to go in feet first…" he said, smiling, "there's a bit of a drop."

Gabi watched as Logan turned face down and slid his feet into the opening. He pushed himself backwards until his whole body disappeared from view. Then she heard his voice: "Come on down!"

Gabi knelt with her back to the entrance and slid her feet in the same way she had seen Logan do it. Her feet had barely passed the threshold of the tunnel when she realised they were over a void.

"There are steps in the wall," Logan said, "just let your legs dangle."

Gabi followed his instructions and allowed her legs to drop into the hole. She felt around with her left foot and found a foothold. A rudimentary ladder had been carved into the stone wall and she slowly made her way to the bottom, where she found herself standing in a narrow tunnel. The ceiling was very low and Logan had to stoop to stay upright.

Yuri carefully made his way down the steps to join

the other two in the corridor as Logan pulled his phone from his pocket and turned on the torch. "This way," he said, turning right, "it's not very far."

They walked through the dark stone passage for about two or three minutes, hindered only by the spiderwebs hanging from the ceiling. It was clear no one had been down there in a long time. "I used to come down here when I was newly ordained," Logan said as they walked, "If we had gone left, it leads out to a hidden entrance in the cloisters at the back of the cathedral. But I always thought it was strange that this direction seems to come to a dead end, roughly under the white stone at the Cathedral's intersection…"

His words trailed off as they reached a large stone wall. Unlike the walls either side of them, made up of many smaller rocks and boulders, this wall was one large slab of smooth grey stone. Other than being one piece, there was nothing else remarkable about it. No markings. No inscriptions. Nothing to indicate it was anything but a rock.

Gabi took a couple of steps closer, "There's got to be a way through," she said, "at least, if this is the right place." She placed her hands on the wall and leaned her ear against it, listening.

"Gabi!" Yuri's voice pierced the silence, "Look! Turn your torch off Logan!" he added.

Logan turned his torch off and the corridor was bathed in a soft blue-white light. Gabi stepped back abruptly and the light dimmed to nothing.

"I think it's the pendant," Yuri said, "go back to the wall."

Gabi took a step forward and a faint light started emanating from under her hoodie. Reaching for her pendant she pulled it out so the light was no longer hidden. Another step closer and the light grew brighter still, filling the enclosed passage with an eerie light. One more step and they were bathed in light as bright as sunshine.

"What's that?" Logan said, pointing at the wall.

In the pendant's bright light, words had formed on the stone slab in front of them – shadows cast by the smallest of imperfections on the surface of the stone. They read:

A espada dos anjos se esconde aqui
Escondido seguro para alguém de coração puro
Quando as sombras entrarem, a chama ela produz
Pois a escuridão não existe onde se encontra uma luz

"I recognise those words!" Gabi said, "I think it's the same words my great-great-grandfather saw on the rock where the stone was hidden."

"But how do we get to it?" Logan said.

"I don't know," Gabi replied.

She leaned in closer, putting her face flat against the wall again, watching, as with every slight movement, shadows seemed to dance across the surface of the wall. Each shadow, each letter, seemed to flicker as she moved the pendant. Except one.

Directly in the centre of the wall a single dark circle had appeared. It didn't move no matter where Gabi stood.

Reaching out she placed her finger on it. It was a small indentation, about a centimetre deep, and roughly one and a half centimetres in diameter. "I think we need a key," she said, "any ideas?"

"I've got a feeling I know exactly what will open this," Yuri said, "May I?"

Gabi nodded as Yuri gently lifted Gabi's necklace from around her neck. He placed the pendant in the hole in the door and for a moment the corridor went dark again. There was a loud cracking, followed by the sound of grinding stone, as the stone wall in front of them started to slide backwards. Yuri removed the pendant from the wall and handed it back to Gabi, filling the corridor with light again.

The stone had moved, revealing a hidden chamber, bathed with light, and there, in the very centre of the room, floating in midair above a stone platform, was the most incredible sword she had ever seen.

About four-foot-long from the end of the handle to the tip of the blade, the hilt was made of gold, covered in jewels, and the grip itself was black leather. The double-edged blade seemed to shimmer with a light all of its own.

In awe, Gabi took a step towards it.

"We've found it," she said quietly, "We've actually found it!"

She reached up and wrapped her fingers around the grip. Immediately they were plunged into darkness. Logan fumbled for his phone and turned the torch on again.

Gabi examined the sword up close. It was remarkably light in her hands, and was perfectly balanced. On the bejewelled guard she noticed a missing gap in the intricate decoration. "I guess this is where you took the gem for my pendant from?" she said to Yuri.

He looked closer, his eyes watery. "Yes, it is," he whispered, "I remember it as if it were yesterday…"

His voice trailed off into the distance, captivated by the memory. Then Yuri shook his head, "Sorry… How are we going to get it out of here? It's not like we can carry a sword through the Cathedral with all those tourists there," he said.

"It'll look less obvious in this," Logan said, reaching towards the wall on their left. Hanging there was a dark brown leather scabbard. He picked it up and wiped the cobwebs off with the end of his sleeve before handing it to Gabi who slid the sword inside and slung the strap over her shoulder.

"We'll head out into the cloisters," Logan said, "It should be starting to get dark soon, so hopefully no one will see us. Follow me." He turned and led the way out of the chamber.

As Gabi left the chamber, the stone door slid into place and the room was sealed again.

She followed Logan's torch light, back into the darkness.

Forty miles away, Harriet and Melchiriel were startled out of an uncomfortable, exhausted silence by the sound of a blood curdling scream.

Damriel's voice, screaming in rage: "She's found it. She's bloody found it. Don't let her get back here!"

They felt the force of a hundred silent shadows rushing out the room and, for the first since they had been captured, they felt a glimmer of hope.

The Cloisters at Winchester

CHAPTER THIRTY-SIX

Logan cracked open a dusty wooden door at the end of the long passage. He stuck his head out, looked left and right, then said: "Come on. Looks clear."

He opened the door fully and stepped out onto a cobbled path running between two parts of the cathedral. Gabi and Yuri followed him, Gabi taking hold of Yuri's hand to help him down the two stone steps onto the path.

Logan had been right. It was starting to get dark. Twilight had set in and the evening was at that point where the sun was below the horizon but still fighting to shine a little light. The street lamps were just starting to turn on around the Cathedral grounds.

"It's this way," Logan said, heading right towards an open area of lawn, hidden from the sight of anyone at the front of the cathedral. "We shouldn't be spotted here."

They walked hurriedly along the path around the lawn as the sky darkened, starlight starting to break through the clouds, blue giving way to black. The path ran between medieval stone buildings. Gabi noticed lights in some of the windows, as residents of the ancient city went about their evening routines, some watching television, some reading, some simply tidying up. None of them aware of the incredible relic she was carrying, as surreptitiously as possible, through the dark streets outside.

In the distance a dog barked and a car horn sounded as tyres screeched to a halt. There were voices shouting in the night. Gabi couldn't make out what they were saying, but they sounded angry. The jewel on her pendant had started to glow. She looked to her right, in the direction from which she'd heard the shouting. There was a gap in the wall through which she could see the lawned area at the front of the Cathedral.

A shirtless man was sprinting across the grass. Sweat glistened on his sinewy body as he ran, barefoot, directly towards them. Slightly ahead of him a small brown dog bounded along, foam forming around its open mouth.

"Run!" Gabi shouted, breaking into a sprint away from the running man. Yuri and Logan followed as several doors burst open and people streamed from the buildings out onto the street around them.

"It's Damriel's army!" Yuri shouted, "He's using them all! Don't let them get the sword!"

The three ran as fast as they could towards an archway at the far end of the courtyard leading out onto the street where their car was parked. Behind them an army of dead eyed soldiers gave chase. People of all different ages, genders, and sizes, followed them at speed.

"Almost there!" Gabi shouted.

As she did, the same white Toyota screeched to a stop in the road through the archway ahead of them. The side door slid open and the two twins, dressed in their non-matching clothing, climbed out, their parents just behind them. Their eyes were empty and black as they lumbered through the archway towards them, blocking their escape.

Logan suddenly cried out in pain. Gabi turned to see him being attacked by a man in priest's clothing. She immediately recognised the priest. It was Rupert, who they had met at the door to the cathedral only a few hours ago. Rupert's eyes were dark and hollow as his arms flailed, grabbing at Logan who had both hands on the possessed priest's shoulders. Logan put his right leg back to stop himself from being pushed over by his old friend when Rupert suddenly pulled back. Logan lost his grip and Rupert rushed at him. Seemingly from out of nowhere Logan's right fist swung, connecting with the left side of older priest's jaw. Rupert fell back, his head hitting the floor with a sickening thud.

Meanwhile, the shirtless man's dog had just reached Yuri. It let out a yelp as Yuri kicked it away. The dog flew through the air, landing on the grass, dazed. At this, the shirtless man grabbed both sides of Yuri's head with his curled fingers and pulled him towards his frothing mouth with a ferociousness Gabi had only ever seen in horror movies. The man ripped a chunk of flesh from Yuri's neck with his teeth, his face now covered in blood.

Before she could react, Gabi was thrown to the floor. The two twins were on top of her, pinning her down. Tracksuit Twin was punching her over and over in the face. She felt each blow land hard, her head being knocked left then right. There was a sharp pain in her side as the other twin stood over her, kicking her in the ribs and stomach. Panic started to set in as Gabi tried to curl into a ball, her hands raised to protect her face.

Behind her, Yuri kicked the shirtless man's shins and shoved him hard in the chest. The man flew back across the Cathedral grounds, his back snapping on the trunk of an old oak tree. He did not get up again.

"Logan!" Yuri shouted as he ran towards Gabi, "We've got to get Gabi!"

Logan didn't hear him. Rupert's body still lay on the floor where he had fallen, but a teenage boy, a middle-aged woman, and two older men had forced Logan to the floor. They were pinning him to the ground, punching and kicking him. Logan's arms were up in front of him as he tried to push them off, but he simply wasn't strong enough. Blow after blow rained down on him.

Yuri grabbed hold of Tracksuit twin and pulled him away from Gabi, swinging him into the other twin, sending them both flying, their bodies bouncing across the cobbled road. He grabbed Gabi's hand and pulled her to her feet just as a large forearm wrapped around his neck. The twin's father's grip was strong and their mother joined him, kicking Yuri hard in the chest. All the air was knocked out of him as his legs gave way. As the grip around his neck tightened, blackness started to creep into the edges of his vision.

The crowd of the possessed had now fully surrounded them, and as the light started to fade in Yuri's eyes he said: "The sword, Gabi!"

Two burly men with shaved heads, eyes completely taken by the shadows, were walking towards her. Out the corner of her eyes she could see more of Damriel's soldiers closing in. Despite the paralysing fear, something instinctive kicked in and her right hand reached over her shoulder and took hold of the ancient sword's hilt. In one movement she pulled it from its scabbard and the whole courtyard was filled with bright white light.

For a moment, everything was suddenly still.

Then, one by one, the Army of Shadows turned their heads towards her and, with a scream that made her blood run cold, they sprinted towards her.

The sword's blade burst into flames and without thinking Gabi swung it.

A wave of bright blue fire shot across the courtyard. She heard scream after scream as shadow after shadow abandoned their hosts, fleeing for their lives. Every shadow touched by the flame was instantly consumed.

And then, as quickly as it had appeared, the flame was gone.

Around her the street was littered with the host bodies that moments earlier had been intent on killing them. Gabi ran over to where Yuri was lying. His face was swollen and bleeding, both his eyes almost closed from the swelling around them, his skin was black and blue.

He reached his hand up to her face: "Are you ok?" he asked.

"I think so," Gabi said, "but you don't look too good."

"I don't feel great," the old angel said, "but I'll be ok... Where's Logan?"

Gabi looked across the road to see Logan pushing himself up from the floor. His face was also battered and bruised, but he could still stand. He walked across to where Rupert lay on the floor. Logan crouched and paused for a moment. He put his hand on the priest's shoulder and whispered: "I'm so sorry my friend."

Logan made his way across the street towards Gabi. "He's still breathing," he said, "but he needs an ambulance."

"I'm sure there's one coming. We need to get out of here," Gabi said, "Can you help me with Yuri?"

Logan reached down, sliding his arm under Yuri's armpit and around his back. Gabi did the same and, between them, they slowly made their way out of the courtyard into the backstreets of Winchester City.

In the distance they heard the sound of sirens as police and ambulance rushed towards them.

They lay Yuri across the back seat of Logan's car and set off into the night.

The River

CHAPTER THIRTY-SEVEN

"We need to get him to a hospital," Logan said, driving as fast as the city's one-way system would allow him, "The Royal Hampshire County Hospital is just around the corner!"

"We can't go to a hospital. They'll find us."

"But he's bleeding…"

Gabi felt a sense of resolve she hadn't felt before. Something had shifted in her. She could feel it. An unexpected sense of purpose. A strength she hadn't known she possessed.

"Find me some water. A fountain. A stream. Anything."

"I know a place," Logan replied, "It's a little bit off the beaten track though."

"Sounds perfect," Gabi replied.

Logan drove the car towards the motorway, heading out of the City before turning left down a narrow winding road with no pavement. They drove past old houses with doors that opened directly onto the road itself, before reaching a humpback bridge. He pulled into a small car park on the right-hand side. It was empty.

He stopped the car at the far end of the car park, as far from the road as he could get, right next to a footpath that led into the woodland. Gabi could hear the sound of running water.

"They use this river for kayaking and canoeing during the day, but it should be fairly empty now that it's dark," Logan said.

"Perfect. We need to get Yuri down to the water," Gabi said, "And we need to do it fast."

Logan opened the rear passenger door as Gabi hid the sword in the boot of the car.

Yuri wasn't moving. A dark red stain had spread across his shirt, almost completely hiding its original colour. "Come on," Logan said, "You take his legs."

Logan reached in and put his hands under Yuri's arms, pulling him gently out of the car. Gabi took hold of his legs, shut the car door behind them, and they carried their injured friend into the woods.

The darkness of the night and the shelter of the trees hid them from view as they carried the unconscious angel along the footpath. They had only walked for about three minutes when, just over forty metres from the car park, they came to a clearing by the water's edge.

"Put him in the water," Gabi said, "I think I can heal him."

They carried their friend into the river and lowered him carefully into the shallow water. The water was cold as it rushed past, turning red as it washed the blood from Yuri's wounds.

"I healed myself in a McDonald's in London," Gabi said, crouching down by Yuri's head, "And all I had to do was splash water on my wounds… I hope this works."

She cupped her hands together and filled them. In the darkness she could see her hands were glowing faintly under the water. She poured the water on Yuri's head and the cuts and bruises on his forehead and cheeks almost instantly closed up as his skin seemed to stitch itself back together.

Yuri groaned and his eyes opened.

"It's working!" Logan exclaimed, "It's actually

working! Focus on his neck. That's his biggest injury."

Blood was still oozing from where the shirtless man had ripped chunks of flesh from Yuri's neck. Gabi poured more water from her hands over the wound and watched as the edges of the wound started to slowly close up.

"Where... where are we?" Yuri's quiet voice whispered into the night.

"We're still in Winchester," Gabi replied, "I'm just trying to make you better. You've lost a lot of blood."

"Have you still got the sword?" Yuri's voice was faint.

"Yes. It's safe." Gabi poured another handful of water over Yuri's injury but the healing seemed to have slowed.

"Good. That's good," the old angel replied, "There's no one more deserving. You are stronger and wiser than you know..."

Blood was flowing faster from the wound now. Every cupped handful of water Gabi poured on it seemed to just wash more blood downstream.

"Come on!" Gabi whispered, "Come on. Please. Please work."

Yuri reached up his right hand and gently took hold of Gabi's, his grip weak. His pale eyes stared straight into hers.

"Tell my Naomi I love her," he whispered, his eyes closing, "tell her I..."

His voice trailed off as his fingers lost their grip, his hand sliding slowly into the water as he breathed out one final time.

"No," Gabi said, "No! Don't go. Don't you dare leave me. Don't you dare!"

She wrapped her arms around him and pulled him close, holding him tight. "How dare you?" she shouted, staring up at the stars, "How dare you?"

Logan crouched down beside her and put his arm around her shoulders, silent as the heavens above them.

Tears streamed down her face, as Gabi looked down

at the face of the old man she now held in her arms, the wrinkles around his eyes telling a story thousands of years old. A story of struggle and surrender, of sorrows and joy, of life, and death, and love. This cursed angel who chose love over strength and status, had welcomed her into his life. He'd made her feel safe. And now he was gone.

The sound of hundreds of birds taking flight from the trees around them shattered the stillness, followed by a rushing wind. The wind seemed to flow along the river, circling around them, pulling at Gabi's hair and clothes, and then, as quickly as it started, everything was still again.

In her hands were Yuri's bloodstained clothes.

His body, however, was gone.

Standing slowly, she turned to Logan, her voice barely audible:

"Let's go," she said, "It's time to end this. Damriel's going to pay for what he's done."

King Edward's School, Capel Cross

CHAPTER THIRTY-EIGHT

The drive to Capel Cross was uneventful. Leaving Winchester at nine-thirty at night meant the country roads Logan chose to take were quiet, even if the lower speed limits meant the journey took an hour, instead of the forty minutes it would have taken on the motorway.

"This way we're less likely to be seen," Logan said, "or attacked."

Gabi nodded. She didn't feel like talking, so for the rest of the journey neither of them said a word.

Turning into Capel Cross High Street just after ten-thirty, Gabi felt a sadness she hadn't expected. This was where she had grown up. It should feel like home and yet it felt distant. It felt like somewhere that belonged in someone else's story. It would never be the same. Her aunt and uncle were dead. Her home was gone. Rafa was missing.

An eerie stillness seemed to have fallen on the village. There were only two cars in the pub car park, where normally at this time it would be full. There was no one out in the streets, and while the village streets weren't normally very busy at this time of night, Gabi would have expected to see at least one dog walker, or someone stumbling home drunk from The White Stag. Tonight, she saw no one.

"Pull in here," Gabi said, breaking the silence.

Logan pulled into a car park outside a community centre next to a large field.

"Rafa plays football here on Sundays," Gabi said, "and we used to play on those swings when we were little."

She paused for a minute and then shook her head as she snapped out of the memory, returning to the present.

"We need to work out where Damriel might be keeping Rafa and the others," she said, "and I haven't had a chance to look at the school map I 'borrowed'."

"The map?" Logan asked.

"I guess Yuri didn't tell you?" Gabi said, "It's an old architect's plan of my school. We know Damriel's keeping Rafa and the others at the school, and we found out there are secret tunnels under there, so we figured he must be keeping them somewhere under the school, otherwise they'd have been found by now."

"That makes sense," Logan said, "do you know how to get in to the tunnels?"

"No, not yet," she replied, "that's what the map's for. Can you pop the boot?"

Logan pressed a button on the dash and the boot of the car clicked open. Gabi got out and went around to the back of the car, swung the boot door up and reached in. She slung the sword in its scabbard over her shoulder and took the map out of her bag.

She carried it round to the front of the car and spread it open on the bonnet.

"Can I borrow your phone?" she asked, "mine's on 11% battery."

Logan pulled his iPhone out of his pocket and handed it to Gabi. She turned on the light on the back of the phone and shone it at the map, staring intently.

"I know it's near the archway at the front of the school somewhere..." she said, examining the map, "There it is. It's in the main block, the same block where Mr Cox's office is."

"Who's Mr Cox?" Logan asked.

"The Headmaster," she replied, "It's at the front of the school, near all the admin offices."

"We heading up there now?" Logan said.

"Yes," Gabi replied, "But we need to leave the car here. It'll attract too much attention. No one drives into the school at this time of night."

"And I guess they'll be looking for you?"

"Yeah. I guess," Gabi replied, "We can't let anyone see me."

"We better get going then," Logan said, "It's going to take a while to get there. We must be about a mile away from the school."

"Don't worry about that," Gabi said, folding the map back up and shoving it in her back pocket, "Give me your hand."

Logan held out his hand and Gabi took it firmly in hers.

"Ready?" she asked, with just the suggestion of a twinkle in her eye.

Before Logan even had a chance to reply he saw a flash of light and they were standing by the road outside the grand façade of King Edward's School, Capel Cross.

"Wha…? What just happened?" he stuttered.

"It's a Nephilim thing… I don't fully understand it properly yet… but come on, we need to find a way in."

Gabi led the way as they walked through the large entrance gate on the left-hand side of the building. The driveway leading up to the impressive Edwardian school building was wide enough for two cars. A well-manicured lawn with just a single tree separated the school from the main front gates and the main road. A white stone cross on a pedestal stood at the edge of the lawn marking the centre point of the building, a reminder of the school's Christian heritage.

"Quick! We don't want to be seen," Gabi said.

"Isn't there CCTV?" Logan asked.

"No," she replied, "I don't think they're allowed it.

Filming children at school is generally frowned upon..."

Sticking close to the left-hand side of the drive they quickly made their way to the archway in the centre of the building. There was no movement anywhere. The whole building was in darkness other than the lights illuminating the stone cross. Ducking under the archway Gabi ran up the three steps to the door that led into the Headmaster's Corridor and tried the handle.

"It's locked."

"Is that another way in?" Logan was looking across at the door the other side of the archway.

"No, that just leads to the other side of the building. I don't know if there's a way round from that side and the map says the entrance to the tunnels is on this side."

"We'll have to try the windows," Logan said.

Gabi followed him as he went through the archway into the part of the school known as the "Quad". The statue of King Edward VI still stood there, staring out at them from his pedestal in the centre of the four-sided courtyard. She'd always thought it was creepy.

The windows were large sash windows that opened upwards from the bottom, set in a row along the ground floor behind a flower bed.

"I'll start at the other end," Logan said hurrying to the far end of the building.

The first window Gabi tried didn't budge. Nor did the second one. The third window lifted about two inches before getting stuck.

"Here!" Logan said in a hushed whisper, "This one's open!"

Gabi rushed over to where he was standing. The window into the office was wide open. "I'll give you a leg up," Logan said, crouching and locking his fingers together so she could use them as a step up into the building.

She put her foot on his hands and climbed through the window into the dark office.

"Come on, it's clear," she said as Logan pulled

himself up onto the window sill, "I think it's the Old Capellians office. They keep records of everyone who's ever been to the school. But they're only here once or twice a week. They must have forgotten to lock the window. The Head's Corridor is just through that door."

Gabi slowly turned the large bronze door handle, hoping and praying they'd forgotten to lock the door too. There was a click as the latch released and the door opened.

She flinched as the light in the corridor suddenly came on, hurting her eyes. She heard a heavily accented voice she immediately recognised as Mr Morvay. He sounded like he was talking on the phone:

"...so annoying. The headmaster is so paranoid since the break in he makes us patrol the corridors after they're all in bed... I know... I trained to be teacher... not security man..."

Gabi pushed the door to, and watched through the crack as Mr Morvay tried the door to the office at the far end of the corridor, his mobile phone firmly pressed to his ear.

"Anyway," Mr Morvay continued, still engrossed in his conversation, "I need to make locked all the doors... I'll call you later... love you too."

Gabi pushed the door shut as the teacher put his phone in his pocket.

"Shit," she said, "Someone's coming and he's making sure all the doors are locked. We're going to get locked in!"

"Let me see," Logan said. Gabi stood aside and Logan cracked the door open again. The young teacher was now only two doors away. "Pass me that stapler," he said, pointing at a large black stapler on the desk to Gabi's left, "and get ready to run."

Gabi passed him the stapler. He took it with his left hand and stepped back from the door, keeping his right hand on the door handle. He looked at Gabi; "Ready?"

In the corridor Mr Morvay's fingers closed around

the door handle and pressed down. As he did Logan pulled hard, swinging the door open. The teacher stumbled forward, pulled into the room by the door. Logan put his right arm around his neck, getting him into a headlock. With his left hand he jabbed the stapler into the frightened man's rib cage. "Don't scream," Logan hissed, "I don't want to shoot you. Understand?"

The teacher nodded his head.

"Give me your keys and your phone," Logan continued, "Slowly!"

The man pulled a bunch of keys from his right pocket and his phone from his left.

"Give them to my friend," Logan said.

Gabi stepped out from behind the door.

"Gabi!" Mr Morvay said, "Is that you?"

"It's me," she said, taking the phone and keys from his trembling hands, "And I'm really sorry."

"Lock us in," Logan said, "I'll stop him from making any phone calls."

"Don't hurt him, will you?"

"For goodness sake, Gabi, I'm a bloody priest," he replied, "Now go!"

Gabi left the office, stepping into the Headmaster's Corridor, just in time to hear Logan saying "Sit there, and don't move."

She pulled the door shut and found the right key, locking Logan in with the Hungarian teacher.

The map had shown a hidden tunnel leading from the end of the corridor by the exit under the archway, where they had first tried to get in. She turned left and headed to the end of the corridor.

The dark wood paneling lining the walls of the corridor extended from floor to ceiling making the corridor feel much narrower than it actually was. She walked straight to the door at the end of the corridor. The entrance had to be on the left side of the corridor as the right would lead out to the front of the school. She pushed and prodded the wood panels in the space between the final office door on the left and the door out into the Quad. Nothing moved. Not even a millimetre.

She put her hand on one of the Tudor Rose carvings that decorated the door frame around the exit door and remembered the hidden switch in the altar at Guildford Cathedral. Starting at the top of the door frame she meticulously pressed the centre of every one of the decorative carvings. They had clearly been painted over many times, and the white gloss paint was thick. Then she saw it. Tiny cracks around the centre of a Tudor Rose, the second one up from the floor. She crouched down and pressed it with her thumb. An almost inaudible click came from inside the wood panel to her left as it popped outwards ever so slightly.

With the tips of her fingers she pulled the panel open and peered into the darkness beyond. She could just make out some steps leading down into the ground.

She stepped through the opening in the wall, pulled the panel shut behind her and was immediately engulfed in darkness.

CHAPTER THIRTY-NINE

"She's here!" Damriel roared, "She's here! I can feel her. I can practically smell her." His usual clipped British accent was gone, his voice filled instead with a guttural, twisted, anguish that couldn't hide his disdain, his disgust, and perhaps just a little fear.

Harriet and Melchiriel watched as he seemed to grow, his shoulders casting a wider, deeper, longer shadow, his dark suit stretching at the seams. "Find her," he continued, speaking into the shadows around him, "Tell me where she is."

Damriel turned his attention to his two prisoners. "The stupid girl thinks she can save you," he said, "She's an idiot. I'll make sure she gets here just in time to watch you both die. And then I'll get to enjoy the pleasure of killing her myself."

"Don't do this, Damriel," Melchiriel said, "You don't have to do this. It's not what you were created for. It's not who you are."

"What do you know about who I am?" Damriel replied, "*He* created me to worship him, the narcissistic bastard. To worship *him*. Why? Why does he need that? Why should I spend eternity worshiping a self-appointed ruler who's done nothing but create pleasures he then forbade us from enjoying? Why the hell would I do that?"

"You know that's not true," Melchiriel said, "You know that's not why he made us. We were made to bring beauty into a world that needed our light. We were made to shine his light into the darkest corners of infinity. We were made for glory. Our glory was his glory, and his glory ours."

"That's bullshit, and you know it," Damriel said, "We were nothing more than slaves, made to do his bidding and sing song after song about him. And you still peddle his twisted propaganda, even after everything he did to you. He could have saved her. You know he could have saved her and instead he watched as the one person I ever truly loved died. You know that." The demon shook his head, "You need to stop talking now. In fact, you need to stop talking *permanently*."

In the blink of an eye Damriel crossed the room. He lifted Melchiriel's chained body off the floor, looped a chain around his mouth, pulling it tight, trapping Melchiriel's tongue as the chain dug deep into his cheeks and jaw. Blood started to form where the chains cut into his skin. With a strength he had so far hidden, Damriel slammed Melchiriel into the wall of their prison cell. Melchiriel's bones cracked and broke as the stones in the wall crumbled and broke away with the force used, trapping his broken body in the wall itself, halfway between ceiling and floor.

Harriet watched as Melchiriel's head dropped, the white of his eyes filled with blood. He mumbled something indistinguishable then his eyes closed. Harriet saw his body go limp as all his strength left him.

"The fool," Damriel said, turning his attention to Harriet, "Bloody fool... Now. I know *exactly* what I'll be doing with you."

At the far end of a long dark passage, Gabi heard a distant thud. Dust fell from the ceiling onto her head and face. She took out her phone from her pocket and turned on the light on the back. The darkness was so thick the light seemed to fade a matter of feet from her face. There was just enough light to see she was at the top of a steep set of stairs leading down to another narrow corridor. A rope hung from metal loops driven into the brick wall on her left. She held this and started her descent into the black.

At the bottom of the steps her feet found themselves on old stone paving slabs. She shone her phone light ahead but she could see nothing more than thick black. She began walking, sword strapped to her back, her right hand holding her phone, her left running along the cold stone wall, feeling every bump as she went. Every footstep echoed in the dark, the sound of her movements bouncing off the ancient walls. If she stopped walking there was nothing but absolute stillness.

She progressed slowly along the passage. After a while she felt the passage was on a slight incline, but she had no other sense of direction. This could have been leading her anywhere.

Suddenly the pendant around her neck started to glow. There was a rush of wind and she felt something brush past her. Then the faintest of whispers. "He knows you're coming. You're dead now."

Gabi could feel something swirling around her body, knocking the phone from her hand. She heard it smash on the stone floor as her fingers instinctively reached for the sword.

"That won't help," the hushed voices continued, "you're all alone. They're all dead. You're next."

Icy fingers of fear started reaching in to her soul, taking hold of her courage, and strangling her resolve. Her legs started to buckle as her knees shook.

"You can't stop me," Gabi said, her voice stronger than she felt, "Tell him I'm coming."

Her fingers tightened around the hilt and she pulled the sword out. It shone in the darkness as flames flickered along the edges of the blade. For a moment she saw the outlines of the shadows dancing around her, their misfigured faces twisting in the sword's light. As fast as they had arrived, they fled, retreating into the darkness ahead.

Gabi held the glowing sword in front of her and continued her ascent along the long narrow passage way. A few minutes later she heard a door slam, the sound of feet running on stone, and a frightened voice:

"Gabi! Help me! Help me!"

Gabi recognised Harriet's voice immediately. Harriet sounded more afraid than Gabi had ever heard her before. Gabi broke into a run, running straight towards the sound of her voice until she felt Harriet's familiar arms wrap around her, holding her tight.

"Thank god you're here," Harriet said, "I've been so scared."

"It's OK. I've got you now," Gabi said, holding her friend tight, "What happened?"

"I don't want to talk about it," Harriet replied, "Let's just go."

Harriet took Gabi's hand and started back towards the entrance to the tunnel.

"No," Gabi said, "What about the others?"

"They'll be ok. Let's just go."

"No," Gabi replied, pulling her arm back and taking a step away from her friend, "I'm going back for the others. How did you manage to get away?"

"I'm not really sure," Harriet said, "Damriel threw Melc up against the wall and was losing his mind. I think he was distracted and hadn't shut the door properly when he came in. I crept slowly towards the door while he was shouting at Melc, and I guess he didn't see me. I managed to open the door and then I just ran."

"And he didn't see you?"

"I don't think so. Can we just go?"

Harriet took hold of Gabi's hand with both of hers and started pulling again. Gabi ripped her hand back out of her friend's grip. "Stop!" she said. She held up the glowing sword, casting light on Gabi's face, and looked deep into her eyes. "One more question," she said," What song wakes you up in the morning?"

"What?" Harriet said, "What do you mean?"

"What song do you have set as your alarm in the morning? Only the real you would know this."

There was a pause.

Then, with a guttural scream, Harriet launched herself at Gabi, her darkened eyes wide open. Harriet's possessed fingers wrapped around Gabi's throat and squeezed tight. The sword clattered onto the stone slabs, its flame immediately extinguished. Gabi felt the room start to spin and sunk slowly to the floor. "Get…off…" she croaked, "Let… her… go…"

Gabi felt an inky blackness creeping in as her vision started to blur and fade. Gabi's right hand reached up and took hold of Harriet's left thumb and with what strength she had left she twisted. There was a loud crack and Harriet's grip loosened just enough. Gabi punched her friend square in the centre of her chest and her friend flew backwards into the darkness.

She rolled over, scrambling for the sword, until she found the ancient hilt. The moment her fingers touched the handle the blade's flame returned, lighting the corridor in its blue-white flickering light. Gabi heard the same gut-wrenching scream as Harriet darted towards her from the shadows, scuttling across the cold stones on all four at an inhuman speed, her face twisted into an unrecognisable grimace.

Unable to stand, Gabi pushed herself backwards along the floor, her feet slipping as she tried to back away. Harriet launched herself at Gabi, her mouth wide open, arms outstretched, as Gabi closed her eyes, lifted the sword and shouted: "Stop!"

The corridor was immediately ablaze with a flash of brilliant white light. Then silence.

Gabi opened her eyes. In the soft light of the sword's flame she could see her best friend's body lying still, her left hand twisted out of shape. Her breathing was shallow, but she was still alive.

"I'm so sorry," Gabi whispered, "I didn't want to do that."

Gabi carefully arranged Harriet's unconscious body into the recovery position, lying her on her front, one leg raised towards her chest, her left arm out, her right hand protecting her face from the cold floor.

"I'll be back as soon as I can," she whispered, "I promise."

Taking a deep breath, Gabi stood to her feet. She knew what she had to do. There was no longer any doubt in her mind. Damriel had done enough damage. It was time for him to pay. It was time to rescue her friends and put an end to all of this.

With the sword out in front of her, she turned and walked away from her friend, into the darkness, into the unknown.

A few short minutes later, Gabi felt the tunnel level out. The light from the flaming blade fell on a grey wall at the end of the corridor. To its left some rough foot holes had been carved into the stones leading up to a wooden trapdoor. Directly opposite, on the right-hand side, was an ancient wooden door. Its handle was a large iron ring, the kind she had often seen on garden gates, or old castle doors.

She turned the iron ring, lifting the latch, and the door creaked open on its rusty hinges.

"Come in, Gabi," a voice called from inside the room, its perfect British accent enunciating each syllable, "I've been waiting."

CHAPTER FORTY

The pendant around Gabi's neck immediately started glowing bright white. She held her sword high as its flames intensified, casting a flickering white light that made shadows dance around the corners of the room. And there he was.

Standing tall in the centre of the room, Damriel, the fallen angel, was resplendent. His tall muscular frame dominated the small underground room. The pinstripes on his immaculately pressed suit seemed to come alive in the flaming light of the sword. Not a single hair was out of place on his head. "I've been expecting you," he said, "and I'm sorry I had to use these tactics to get you here."

"Where are my friends?" Gabi said, "Where's Rafa?"

"All in good time, young lady, all in good time."

She scanned the room and immediately saw Melchiriel's limp body embedded in the stone wall at the far end.

"What. Have. You. Done?" she said, every word dripping with anger. In one swift motion she attacked. Before Damriel could even blink she had jumped, wrapped her arm round his neck and pulled him to the floor with supernatural strength.

Damriel took hold of her arm and, with a strength

that matched her own, he pulled, throwing her over his head. Her body careened through the air, smashing into an old wardrobe in the far corner of the room. She dropped the sword and fell, sliding across the floor, its flame extinguished.

Dazed, Gabi tried to stand, scrambling as her feet slipped on pieces of the broken wardrobe. She fell back as Damriel launched himself at her again.

With the light from the sword now extinguished, her eyes struggled to adjust to the dark, and she could barely see as Damriel's fists rained down a flurry of blows, punching her in the face, left, right, left, and right again.

She raised her right leg and kicked out. Her foot connected squarely with Damriel's chest, knocking the air from his lungs and sending him flying back across the room. Winded, he somehow managed to land on his feet, struggling to catch his breath.

Gabi took advantage of the pause and pushed herself up onto her feet. She looked around for her sword and turned just in time to see a wooden chair flying towards her head. She put her arm up to protect her face and the chair smashed, spraying chunks of wood all around.

She ran at Damriel, launching herself off her feet into a rugby tackle that took out his legs. His whole body then followed as his head smashed into the stone wall. Out of the corner of her eye something glinted in the light of her pendant. It was her sword, half buried under a pile of wood, remnants of the smashed wardrobe. Turning her back on Damriel's fallen body, Gabi crawled on all fours to grab the sword. Just as her fingers were about to grasp the hilt she felt something take hold of her left ankle and her legs were pulled out from under her. She fell face first to the floor as her body was dragged back across the room.

She rolled and put her hands up to protect her head, then slammed them both down on the floor, propelling herself into the air. Kicking hard, her right foot connected with Damriel's chin, knocking him backwards and they both landed on the floor on their backs. Gabi pushed herself back towards where the sword was, taking hold of it before Damriel could get back up.

The room was immediately flooded in the now familiar flickering bright light as the sword burst into flames again. Gabi sprung to her feet and held the sword out in front of her with both hands, its light dancing across her face.

"It's time to give up, Damriel," she said, "Just give up."

Damriel pushed himself to his feet, his dark eyes glowering at his opponent. "You haven't won, little girl," he said, his voice hushed, "It's you who should be giving up."

As he said this he seemed to grow taller. His shoulders pulled back, his arms wide, as two enormous black wings unfurled, ripping his now disheveled suit jacket to shreds. The dark shadowy wings reached from one side of the room to the other and appeared to absorb the light of the sword. They themselves cast no shadow for they were darkness itself.

He reached his right hand up over his shoulder and, from between his wings, he pulled out a sword. Its black blade reflected no light.

"May I introduce my own weapon," he said, a smile spreading across his bloodied lips, "She's called Shadow Blade and was forged by Lucifer himself. She was his pride and joy until I stole it some centuries ago…"

The blade seemed to suck all hope from the room. In its presence the room was darker, as though the blade itself were somehow able to cast darkness the same way flames cast light. Damriel's Shadow Soldiers flooded the room, swarming through the door and around the edges of the window. They swirled around him, creating a black whirlwind that shook the very foundations of the building, picking up furniture, old books, paper. Anything that wasn't tied down was now flying around the room as the shadows surrounded their master in a protective vortex.

Gabi could barely see, her eyes fighting to stay open. The power of the wind, created by the demons, pushed and pulled at her clothes, trying to force her back towards the wall.

"No!" she cried, "I won't let you win."

She forced her arms to raise her sword higher, then turned the blade over and slammed it down into the ground. A wave of fire surged across the room, vaporising shadows and filling the room with light again. Damriel swung his sword.

Gabi stepped back as the tip of the Shadow Blade glanced off her left shoulder, tearing through her skin. The pain was like nothing she had ever imagined. Icy cold hopelessness flooded her being as blood began to seep into her clothes, a dark stain spreading down her sleeve.

Damriel attacked again, bringing his blade down hard towards her head. Gabi raised the Sword of Flames, blocking the attack. Their blades clashed with a sound like thunder that sent tremors through the building.

She swung her sword in a counter attack, slicing through the front of Damriel's right thigh. The Lord of the Army of Shadows roared, stepping back, raising his own sword again. This time Gabi was ready and deflected the blow.

Damriel stumbled forward as the force of the swing made him put weight on his injured leg. Gabi side stepped him and swung. The fiery blade arched across the demon's back as he bent forward, slicing through the base of his left wing. The shadow wing fell to the ground immobile and the room immediately felt a little less dark. She swung again and the flames took his other wing. Damriel fell to his knees and Gabi seized the opportunity.

She took hold of Damriel's jet black hair, pulled his

head back, and held her blade up to his throat. Flames flickered around his face.

"Where is he?" she said, "where's Rafa?"

"Let me go, and I'll tell you," Damriel said, "I'll tell you."

"Tell me, or I'll finish this now." Gabi pressed the fiery blade to the demon's skin. There was a sickly sizzling sound as the flames burned the fallen angel's flesh.

"Please, don't hurt me," Damriel pleaded, his voice little more than a whisper, "I'll show you where he is. Let me show you."

Gabi loosened her grip a little, moving the blade away from his throat.

Damriel tried to stand.

"Slowly," Gabi said, the blade still firmly pressed against the demon's neck, "Very slowly."

She allowed him to stand, bent over, as she kept her grip on him. Unable to stand on his right leg, Damriel limped across the room towards a pile of old chairs and blankets.

"He's under there," Damriel said, "see for yourself."

In the dancing light she could see a hand sticking out from under the pile of discarded furniture. It was a hand she recognised. A hand she had held since she was a little girl. A hand that had held the same kite string she had in the field by the community centre. The same hand that had pulled her hair when they had argued. The same hand that had comforted her whenever she'd hurt herself or cried.

Rafa's still, unmoving hand.

"No!" she cried. She pushed the demon away and his injured body flew back, smashed into the far wall, then fell, clattering on debris, then silent on the floor. Dropping her sword on the ground next to her she frantically started pulling chairs and blankets from the pile, throwing them behind her like they weighed no more than matchboxes until she uncovered his body.

There he was. Motionless. Not breathing. Dead.

Gabi knelt beside him, cradling his head in her arms as she felt tears forming. Then they poured, falling on the cold skin of Rafa's face. She sobbed as she held him.

"I'm sorry," she whispered, "I'm so sorry."

Then she stopped. She sat up a little and moistened her hands with the tears on her cheeks. Taking his face in her hands she closed her eyes. In the half-light her hands started to glow.

"Come on," she said, then louder, "Come on!"

Rafa's body convulsed as she sent healing wave after healing wave.

Taking her hands away from his face, she stopped to listen. There was no sound.

No breath.

She pounded his chest with her fists.

"Come on! Come back! Come back! I can't lose you too…"

"Oh, but my dear," a familiar British accent whispered in her ear, "you already have."

Damriel was right behind her, his shadow blade raised above his head. He brought the sword down straight towards her head as fast as a bolt of lightning. Gabi flinched as her right hand somehow found the sword she had left on the floor beside her.

And then it was over.

Inches from her face, Damriel stopped moving, the sword of flames in Gabi's hand protruding from his back, its flame burning brightly, then spreading slowly, consuming his body until it fell away and there was nothing left.

The Sword of Flames flickered, the flames went out and, once again, the room was plunged into a still, silent darkness.

Queen Anne House

CHAPTER FORTY-ONE

Gabi sat in silence in the gloom until a pale white light suddenly filled the room and she heard Harriet's voice from the doorway: "Is it over?"

"I think so," Gabi replied. Harriet was holding Gabi's broken phone out in front of her, the light on the back shining into the room, casting a soft light over the debris and destruction.

"I'm so sorry about Rafa," Harriet said, "I wish I could have saved him." Tears streamed down her face as she crouched next to her friend and put her arm around her. In her embrace Gabi sobbed as grief took over and the tears came.

Taking a deep breath, she paused for a moment, wiped her tears away and stood up, putting the sword away. "Shit!" she said, "Melc! Is he ok?"

They rushed over to the wall where Melc's unmoving body was still embedded. Harriet put the smashed phone face down on a shelf and together they carefully pulled him away from the wall and lowered him to the ground.

Harriet one-handedly struggled to pull the chain from his mouth. It had cut into his face. His eyes were swollen and puffy, and his breathing was laboured and slow.

"I might be able to heal him," Gabi said, "but I need some water."

"I'll try to find some," Harriet said.

They were interrupted by an almost inaudible whisper: "You… don't need… water…"

Melchiriel's deep familiar voice was slow, "Trust in… yourself," he said.

Gabi placed her hands on Melchiriel's chest. His t-shirt was dirty and sticky with his blood. She closed her eyes and didn't see the light that filled the room as power flowed from her hands into his injured body, knitting muscle and skin, sewing sinews and tendons together, repairing every part of his broken body.

When she was finished, Melchiriel lay there for a moment and there was silence.

"Thank you, Gabi," he said, "I knew you could do it. You were the only one," he paused again, then added, "Now, shouldn't you heal Harriet's hand too?"

Gabi took Harriet's injured hand in hers and within seconds it was healed. "I'm so sorry Harriet," she said, "I never wanted to hurt you."

"I don't think I was really myself," Harriet replied, with the faintest of smiles, "so don't worry about it."

"What do we do now?" Gabi asked, "We need to get Rafa out of here."

"And Andy," Harriet added.

"Andy's here?" Gabi asked, "I guess that's who the police were looking for when they were in Cox's office."

"Yeah…" Harriet said, "Damriel used him to send that warning, and then must have killed him so no one would find out. He left him in that corner." She pointed to the far corner of the room where Gabi could just about make out the shape of a body lying in the shadows.

"We can't leave them here," Gabi said.

"You have to leave them," Melchiriel said, "and you need to get out of here."

"You're coming too aren't you?" Harriet said.

"No," he replied, "with Damriel's body gone, no

one's going to believe your story. I need to get caught. I need to take the blame for kidnapping you - and killing them."

"You can't!" Harriet said, "They'll lock you up."

"But you'll be free," he replied, "don't worry about me. As long as you're safe. Now, we need to find a way of getting you out of here."

Melchiriel walked over to the door and opened it. "Harriet," he said, "shine your light over here."

Harriet held Gabi's phone up, casting light on the rough steps carved into the stone wall opposite the door.

"Gabi, give me the map," Melchiriel said, "if I've got the map with me, it'll prove I stole it. It'll stop police from looking for anyone else."

"But what are you going to do?" Gabi asked, as she pulled the map from her back pocket and handed it to him.

"I'll head to the other end of the passage and find a way of getting caught."

Melchiriel put a hand on each of the girl's shoulders and looked them in the eyes.

"Gabi," he said, "Your mother would be so proud of you. You are so strong, so brave, and capable of so much more than you give yourself credit for."

Then he turned to Harriet; "And you," he said, "are everything anyone could ask for in a friend."

Both girls threw their arms around him and hugged him.

"Will we see you again?" Gabi asked.

"I don't know for sure," he replied, "but I never say never."

With that he turned his back on them and started walking along the stone passage back towards the Headmaster's Corridor.

The girls watched as he walked into the darkness and faded from view.

Gabi put her feet in the first step carved into the wall and started climbing. The steps led into a narrow tunnel hidden in the darkness, and then, about five or six metres up, her hand felt a wooden trap door. She pushed hard and the heavy wooden door lifted up, knocking something heavy onto the floor above her head.

She climbed through the opening and found herself in the fireplace of a large living room. A large metal grate lay on the hearth on the red carpet next to the fireplace. She immediately knew where she was. She was in Queen Anne House. Specifically, she was in the housemaster's private living room. She had been in here to celebrate the end of Junior School when she was about to leave to go to Senior School.

She climbed out of the fireplace then turned and took Harriet's hand to help her up.

Suddenly a light came on in the hall outside the room.

"Who's there?" a man's voice called.

"Quick!" Harriet said, "Hide the sword!"

Gabi looked around then ducked her head into the fireplace. She reached up above her head and her hands found a ledge inside the chimney. She placed the sword on the ledge and climbed out just in time for the door to burst open. Mr Alvez, their maths teacher, and housemaster at QAH ran into the room.

"What are you doing in here?" Mr Alvez said, a look of both concern and relief on his face, "People have been looking for you for days."

"We've just escaped," Harriet said, "we need help."

Meanwhile, Melchiriel had just stepped through the entrance to the secret passage and now stood on the plush carpet that lined the Headmaster's Corridor. He tried the office doors around him. The first three doors were locked and secure. When he tried the fourth door he heard someone with a strong Eastern European accent shout: "Help! Help! I'm being kidnapped!"

There was a commotion inside the room, then someone started banging on the door, shouting: "Help!

I'm locked in! Let me out!"

Melchiriel ignored it and moved on to the next office as the banging continued. The door opened easily. He walked in, picked up the phone and dialled 999.

"Which service?" the operator asked.

"Police, please," he replied.

A few seconds later another voice came on the line: "Surrey Police, what's your emergency?"

"Hi, I'm at King Edward's School in Capel Cross. Someone's breaking in at the front of the school. They're here right now!" He hung up the phone and took a seat behind the desk to wait.

It can't have been more than five minutes before he heard sirens approaching. Moments later four police officers burst through the door, Tasers drawn. "Get down!" they shouted, "Get down!"

Melchiriel knelt on the floor, put his hands behind his back and allowed himself to be handcuffed.

"He's got the map that was stolen a few days ago!" one of the officers exclaimed, "Right mate, you're under arrest on suspicion of burglary."

Two officers took hold of his arms and led him away to the waiting police van.

In the Old Capellian's office, Logan and Mr Morvay had come to an uneasy truce. The young Hungarian teacher was sat silent in the office chair behind the desk while Logan stood by the door. This was when Logan heard someone in the corridor. He raised his index finger to his lips. The young teacher shrugged and nodded.

Then someone tried the handle to their door. Logan's prisoner jumped up from the chair and shouted: "Help! Help! I'm being kidnapped!"

Logan rushed towards him, putting his hand over his mouth, desperate to keep him quiet. The young teacher shook himself free and ran to the door, pounding on it and shouting: "Help! I'm locked in! Let me out!"

There was nothing Logan could do now, so he climbed back out the window and ran. He turned right, ran under the archway at the front of the school and out onto the main road. Turning left at the road, he ran down the hill towards the centre of Capel Cross village, to the car park where he had left his car. There was no one around and the sound of his footsteps, coupled with his rapidly beating heart, seemed to fill his head until the noise of approaching sirens drowned out everything else. He ducked behind a garden wall as two police cars and a police van drove past at speed, lights flashing, sirens wailing.

When the coast was clear, he walked the rest of the way to his car, started the engine and drove home to London, his head now filled with more questions than answers.

CHAPTER FORTY-TWO

Mr Alvez sat and listened as the two girls told him how they had been kidnapped a few days earlier and locked in a dungeon. His wife, who had joined them, put her arms around them both as they cried, telling them how they had been kept in the same room as Andy and Rafa who were both now dead.

"We need to tell the police," Mr Alvez said, "they're the best people to look into this." He pulled his phone out of his pocket and said: "Oh, Rodney Cox has just messaged the teachers' WhatsApp group… he says someone's been arrested breaking in at the front of the school!"

He dialled the headmaster's number, held the phone to his ear, then said: "Rodney, it's Alex, I've got Gabi and Harriet with me… yes, I just saw your message… they said they were kidnapped… yep, and escaped when their captor forgot to lock the door… yes, I'll keep them here… I told them we had to tell police… OK, see you soon."

He hung up, put his phone away and said: "Helen, can you make the girls another cup of tea? Rodney's on his way over with the police. We've got to wait for them."

Ten minutes later, Mr Cox, the headmaster joined

them in the living room. He had three police officers with him, all frantically taking notes as the two friends told their story again.

Two hours later, the sun was coming up. Gabi was very grateful when Helen Alvez said: "Come on. These two need some sleep. They're shattered. You can ask them more questions once they've had a chance to get some rest."

She ushered the two exhausted school girls through into a spare bedroom with two single beds. "Try to get some sleep, girls," she said, "you've had a traumatic day. You need to rest but you're safe now."

The next few days went by in a flurry of activity. Numerous interminable police interviews where they were asked the same questions time and time again by different officers. They were particularly interested in how they had escaped, and why they thought they had been kidnapped.

Gabi and Harriet's stories never deviated from what they had agreed.

"The man," they said, "told us we must be rich as we go to such an expensive boarding school. He wanted our parents' details so he could ask for a ransom."

"He caught us when we tried to run away from school," Gabi added, "the morning after I ran away from the police station."

"Why did you run away from school?" one of the officers asked.

"Police were saying I had killed someone," Gabi answered, "and I never did. I never would."

At this point, the Detective Chief Inspector interrupted the interview: "I don't know where that came from. None of our police officers have been killed. You did hurt one of them when you pushed him and he fell, but no one's been killed. Who told you that?"

Harriet described the two police officers that had come to her room.

"I don't know any officers that look like that," the DCI said, "It must be some kind of mistake. You're definitely not wanted for murder."

The DCI told them they had found Rafa's body, along with Andy's. He told them they had also found signs of a struggle, scorch marks, and the book that had been taken from the headmaster's safe. "The last time there's any record of that room being used for anything was in the second world war," the DCI said, "when the school used it as a practice bunker for bombing drills. It's been pretty much forgotten since then."

A few days later, Social Services agreed Gabi could live with Harriet whenever she wasn't at school, but only after Mr Cox had confirmed Gabi could become a full-time boarder until she finished her A-levels.

That same day, Mr Cox smiled as he told her: "I've got some great news. The burglar they arrested that night has been charged and remanded to Winchester Prison. He's going to go to court for burglary, kidnapping, and murder! He's also confessed to locking Harriet's grandmother in a pantry, but don't worry, she's fine, she was just a bit battered and bruised."

One Monday morning, three weeks later, Gabi was sat next to Harriet in school assembly. Mr Cox stood up and walked to the lectern.

"Thank you for sharing the sports results, Mrs Todd," he glanced over at the girls' P.E. Teacher, who was taking her seat at the front of the hall, "Now, unfortunately, I have some grave news."

He paused as a murmuring spread across the whole assembled school body. He raised his hands and continued: "As you are all no doubt aware, a few weeks ago we suffered tragic losses here at King Edward's. We lost two of our own to a brutal act of criminality. Firstly I must reassure you all that you are safe. We have increased security standards here at school, as you have no doubt noticed, but I am sad to inform you that I received a phone call from the police this morning. They told me that the man charged with the murders of Rafa Dos Santos and Andrew Powell has somehow escaped custody. He was in prison in Winchester last night, but when they checked his cell this morning he was gone.

They've checked CCTV in the prison and all around the surrounding area, but there's nothing to show where he went, just occasional static on the footage, which police tell me is odd as its all digital nowadays…"

Harriet touched Gabi's arm with her elbow to get her attention. "Do you think...?" she whispered.

"Absolutely," Gabi replied with a quiet smile.

At that precise moment, four-hundred and thirty-one miles away, a tall man with greying hair and an unkempt, stubbly beard walked into a charity shop in Edinburgh. He selected a pair of second-hand jeans, a black t-shirt with a Misfits logo on it, and a pair of black Doc Marten's boots. He paid cash for the items then went into the fitting rooms at the back of the shop. Moments later he walked out into the beautiful Scottish sunshine, leaving behind a set of gray tracksuit trousers, a gray t-shirt, and a pair of black pumps.

He looked up at the bright blue sky and smiled. "Mission accomplished," he said, "time to go."

And with that Melchiriel turned and melted into the crowds of tourists, comedians, and street performers on Edinburgh's Royal Mile.

That night, back in Capel Cross, Gabi felt peaceful as she climbed into bed in her new single room, just across the corridor from Harriet. She smiled as she put her head on her pillow, pulled the covers up to her chin, closed her eyes, and fell asleep.

And, perhaps for the first time in years, there were no more nightmares.

EPILOGUE I

Rev Logan Fry was on a day off. He was making coffee in the kitchen at the back of his house. He had tried to put all the events of Winchester Cathedral behind him. That whole day had seemed like some sort of hellish dream. It was definitely not what he had expected when he had decided to help that young girl with her school project. He definitely wouldn't be doing that again in a hurry.

Of course, he had kept up to date with the news of the child murders in Surrey. He had heard about the man charged with the murders, how he had escaped from prison, and how he was now on the Police most wanted list.

But as the weeks went by news turned to more banal subjects; the latest love island contestant found to be acting inappropriately in a night club, a beloved TV presenter stepping down from his role on breakfast television, another politician found fiddling their expenses – the usual.

Suddenly his phone buzzed and a notification popped up on his screen:

"RING: There is a person at your front door."

He heard the letterbox rattle, which was strange as the postman had already been that morning.

He walked through to his hallway and saw a silver envelope on the floor. There was no stamp and no address.

The front of the envelope simply read:

Logan Fry

He opened the envelope and took out the rather plain card he found inside. There were yellow flowers on the front and it looked like any other generic card you might buy at a petrol station or Tesco Express. Inside was a simple note:

Dear Logan,

Thank you for looking after my many-greats-granddaughter.

I will forever be in your debt.

Yours with honour and respect,

Gabriel

Logan put the card down on the radiator by the front door and opened the Ring Doorbell app on his phone. He played back the footage and saw an old man with bright white hair walking up to his front door. The man looked about eighty years old, possibly more, and on the Ring Doorbell footage he had the most piercing brown eyes Logan had ever seen.

Logan watched as the old man posted the envelope through his door, turned, unfurled his golden wings and, with a flash of light, disappeared.

EPILOGUE II

3 AM.

Queen Anne House was silent and empty.

All the pupils had gone home for the summer holidays. Mr Alvez and his family were enjoying time away in Spain.

So there was no one there to see the shadow glide from the fireplace, across the red living room carpet, and out into the night.

There was no one there to see the bright white glow that followed, lighting the room, for just a moment, before fading away again.

And perhaps this was for the better.

I HOPE YOU HAVE ENJOYED THIS BOOK

Thank you for reading my very first novel! I am honoured and humbled that you have given your time to enter the world of the Last Nephilim.

If you have enjoyed this book, (and even if you haven't!) please could you leave an honest review on Amazon?

This helps other people discover the book, and helps me find out what people like and what they don't, so I can improve my storytelling in the future.

Leaving a review is very easy to do and should only take a couple of minutes.
Just scan the QR code below and follow the onscreen instructions.

And again, thank you!

Alex B.

WOULD YOU LIKE ANOTHER?

If you've enjoyed this book and would like to get your hands on another story of the Nephilim *(for FREE!)* simply scan the QR code below and follow the on screen instructions and I will send you a new story straight to your inbox!

ABOUT THE AUTHOR

Alexander J Boxall *(Alex, to everyone but his mum!)*, grew up in Brazil until he was thirteen when he went to boarding school in England, hence a lot of the inspiration for this book. He has written other books, both under his own name and under a pen-name, but this is his very first fiction novel.
He currently lives in Southampton with his family where he is already working on ideas for the next instalment in The Chronicles of the Nephilim.

For more information about Alex and any future publications, please visit www.alexboxall.co.uk.

Printed in Great Britain
by Amazon